THE TEEWINOT CAFE

THE TEEWINOT CAFE

CHINLE MILLER

Yellow Cat
PUBLISHING

Cover by Cary Cox

Next to end photo of the Teewinot Cafe by Chinle Miller

End photo of Teewinot Mountain by Ron Tubbs

For Dash

1

Emery County Sheriff Bud Shumway closed the door to his office, having had it open a crack to let in the cool morning air, though now that it was almost noon, things were heating up.

He'd just sat back down at his desk when the door opened again and his geologist friend, Shorty Doyle, walked in, leaving it open a crack.

"It might cool things down if you left the door open a bit," Shorty informed Bud with a grin, having seen him just close the door.

"Morning, Shorty," Bud replied. "Coffee?"

"Sure," Shorty replied.

"Cream?"

"Sure, but stay put. I can get it."

Shorty poured himself a cup from the coffeepot on a nearby small table, then took a carton of half-and-half from Bud's mini fridge, pouring some into the cup. Sitting down opposite Bud, he pulled a second chair over and put his feet up on it, Bud noting that his worn hiking boots had seen better days.

"Wanna go on a trip?" Shorty asked.

"Sure," Bud replied. "Where are we going?"

"A tad north."

"How far is a tad?"

"A few hundred miles."

"Fishing up at Flaming Gorge?"

"Keep going."

Bud hesitated. It actually sounded nice to go fishing at Flaming Gorge, even though he didn't fish. It was starting to get too hot to do much outside for most of the day, and the reservoir was in Utah's Uinta Mountains, where he figured it would be nice and cool. He could sit under a tree and watch Shorty fish.

Bud fiddled with a pen, tapping it against the rim of his coffee cup, thinking, then said, "Further north would put us up in Wyoming. Not much up there but sagebrush and wind, unless you want to go to Yellowstone."

"Not Yellowstone," Shorty replied.

"Anybody else going on this little trip with us?" Bud asked.

"Not that I know of, though we could invite Howie."

Bud grinned. "Let's see—Howie, who's mayor, and me as sheriff—if you also were some kind of Green River official, we could have a junket. Who's paying for this trip, anyway?"

Shorty answered, "Actually, Bud, believe it or not, the Park Service is going to foot the bill."

"The Park Service? But not Yellowstone?"

"Close, but no cigar."

"The Tetons?"

"Bingo. You just won a free trip."

"The Tetons sound nice and cool. It's supposed to break 100 degrees here today. But how long is this trip going to be, and when?"

"We can leave as soon as you're ready. I don't know how long I'll be up there, but you can come back whenever you want, if we take your FJ. I can figure out my own way back, probably rent a car. They'll buy all the gas. They're providing a Park Service vehicle we can run around in while there, plus food and lodging. And my consulting fee, of course."

"Your fee? You're getting a free trip plus a fee? Should I suspect that there's more to this free trip than meets the eye?"

"Probably," Shorty laughed. "But it would be a good chance for you to do some photography. No place like the Tetons, you know."

Bud grinned. "Is Cassie going?"

"No, she's too busy with her garden, plus she doesn't want to leave Whiskerbiscuit, her cat, and someone needs to take care of Patches."

Shorty hesitated, then pulled his feet off the chair and sat up straight, looking serious. "In all honesty, Bud, I didn't invite her."

"One of those deals, eh, Shorty?" Bud asked. "I take it the park's not hiring you just to do a little geology, especially since they probably have their own staff geologist and you're supposed to be retired."

Shorty shook his head. "The park superintendent is a friend from way back when I taught at Stanford, back before I worked for the Yukon Geologic Survey. I told him I wanted you to come along, and he agreed, after I mentioned your detective skills. It may be something, or maybe not. And don't forget Lindie."

Bud replied, "What exactly is going on? Something that requires a geologist, a lawman, *and* a search and rescue dog?"

Just then, the door opened, and Howie walked in, saying, "A geologist and a lawman walk into a bar with a SAR dog...was the mayor invited? What's going on, fellas?"

"Wanna go on a trip?" Shorty asked.

"Someplace north," Bud added.

"Alaska?" Howie asked. "I've always wanted to go to Alaska."

"Scale it back south a couple of thousand miles," Shorty replied.

"Canada?" Howie asked.

"Go south a tad more," Bud offered.

"Mexico?"

"Now go north," Shorty said.

"Hows about Flaming Gorge? Man, it would be a good day to go fishing there. Too dang hot here," Howie replied, closing the door. "You should keep the door shut, Sheriff. You're letting all the hot air in."

Bud laughed. "Shorty here is offering us a free trip up to the Tetons, Howie, but I think there's some kind of catch to it."

"I'm game, catch or not," Howie replied. "Things at the drive-in are slow, and this heat's getting to me. But Sheriff, I just now had to do your job for you while you sit here drinking coffee with Shorty."

"How so?" Bud asked.

"Well, I just rescued this woman named Marilyn who was lost. That's your job, Bud, you know, SAR—search and rescue—you and Lindie."

"What happened?" Bud asked patiently.

"She was sitting on a dead-end street over on the other side of the river, kind of by the railroad bridge, over in the old part of town called Elgin. I stopped to see if she needed help, and she told me her GPS had gotten her lost. She was trying to find her way back to the freeway."

"It's pretty hard to get lost in Green River," Shorty noted. "She must've been from the city."

"Why would you say that?" Bud asked.

Shorty replied, "Because people from the city are used to chaos and mayhem. They come to Green River and their brains can't deal with the quiet. They get all discombobulated."

Howie continued. "She said she thought she'd about figured her way out by sitting there and looking around and using logic, which wasn't too difficult since you can see the freeway from about everywhere in town." He paused, then asked, "Anyway, how long would we be gone?"

"Like I was telling Bud," Shorty replied. "You can come back whenever you want. I basically just want someone to provide some perspective and help in an investigation the park's hired me to do."

"Sounds pretty serious," Howie said.

"It could be," Shorty said. "Or not. But fellas, it could get complicated and possibly even be dangerous. I want you to be aware of what you may be getting into. I don't know many details, but the park super, Cameron Olsen, has told me two things: one, the park possibly has a new major fossil find, and two, the park geologist, who went up to the site has gone missing. He wants me to take a look at this new site to see if it's legit or not—the problem is, they're not sure where it is. The park LEOs are on the case, and search parties have been looking for the geologist, a guy named Marty Langford. They're not sure if there was foul play or not, and Cam doesn't want me going up there alone, so I decided to invite you guys along."

"Much appreciated," Howie said sarcastically. "Will there be gunplay?"

Bud replied, "Howie, if I had a nickel for every time you asked that..."

Howie said, "You'd have about 15 cents, Sheriff. One needs to be prepared, you know that better than anyone—you taught me that when I was your deputy. But why not have one of the rangers go up with you, Shorty?"

"He doesn't want word to get out about the fossils," Shorty replied. "Like I said, it could be a major find, the kind looters would love. This is all going to be on the hush-hush."

Howie asked, "Is this going to require some heavy-duty hiking? If so, I need some new boots."

"Me, too," Bud added. "My Herman Survivors probably wouldn't survive."

"Does that mean yes?" Shorty asked.

"I can arrange for the state patrol to cover for me," Bud replied. "And you, Howie?"

"Count me in," Howie said. "I'll bring my telescope. The night sky up there should be fantastic. I'm going to shut down the drive-in for a week or two. That way, Maureen can take a break while I'm gone."

"What about your mayoral duties?" Bud asked.

Howie replied, "As long as we get back for Rockabilly Night, nobody will even miss me. Let's see...we have three weeks until the next one."

Shorty replied, "We're going to be staying in Alta, a little town of around 300 people."

"I've heard of Alta," Howie said. "It's the only town in Wyoming that you can't get to *from* Wyoming."

"How would that work?" Bud asked.

"It's on the west side of the Tetons, so can only be accessed from the west, which is Idaho," Howie replied. "Though I guess you could access it from the east if you wanted to climb over the Tetons."

Shorty added, "It's a place called the Teewinot Cafe—Teewinot after the big peak over by the Grand Teton."

"We're going to stay in a cafe?"

"No, it used to be a cafe. Before that, it was a small ski lodge, and now it's a resort rental. It's a landmark in Alta. What say we meet at Bud's at eight tomorrow morning?"

"Sounds like a plan," Bud replied. "And let's hope we only have to deal with one missing geologist, not two, Shorty. We need to agree to a plan to keep it that way."

"We definitely don't need any more lost people," Howie added. "I hope that gal Marilyn's not going up there. She'd for sure get lost in the Tetons."

Shorty nodded as they all walked out the office door, Bud locking it behind them.

2

Bud woke with a start. He knew instantly that something was wrong, and he instinctively reached for his Ruger on the nightstand next to his bed, but it wasn't there. In fact, the nightstand wasn't there either and appeared to have been replaced by some kind of small dresser with drawers.

He could hear growling coming from the foot of the bed and knew it was Lindie, though he couldn't understand why she wouldn't be in her dog bed on the floor, where she always slept.

He could tell it was dawn from the dim light coming through the window, which appeared to be on the wrong side of the room, and as he sat up a bit, he could now see what Lindie was growling at—something huge and dark was looking in the window!

Puzzled that his gun wasn't where he swore he'd left it, he slipped out of bed and into his slippers, carefully staying to the side of the room away from the window, making his way to the bedroom door, quietly calling Lindie to follow, then slipping into the hallway.

Now Bud could hear voices coming from another part of the house, and he realized he wasn't home in Green River after all, but was in the rental he and Howie and Shorty had arrived at late the previous night, the Teewinot Cafe, as the sign above the front door reminded them.

It had been built in what Bud knew was called the Swiss Alps style, a chalet with a story and a half, and a pitched roof with front gables and wide eaves supported by decorative brackets. The deck railings and windows also had decorative trim with heart and tree cutouts, and along the front of the house was a hand-carved wooden sign that read: *Wander, but wherever you roam, be happy and healthy and glad to come home.*

Bud had instantly liked the house, though he hadn't had much time to explore it. A brochure had said it was built as a lodge in 1971, shortly after Grand Targhee opened. It was an outpost for the Grand Targhee ski team and saw many famous and infamous guests through the years. It had eventually been turned into a cafe, then remodeled into a resort rental, the small bedrooms made into larger ones.

Shorty and Howie were now coming to see what was going on, and Bud, having finally persuaded Lindie to follow him, met them in the kitchen.

"She's barking at that moose outside," Shorty said. "Bad doggie, Lindie. Those guys can be mean, and they hate dogs, so you'd best stay away from them. They associate dogs with wolves, which threaten their calves."

"It's kind of an interesting way to wake up," Bud replied. "Your dog is growling, your gun is missing, and something huge is looking in your window."

"Nice PJs," Howie grinned. "Scooby-Doo all the way, eh? But what happened to your gun?"

"It was the victim of sleep confusion," Bud replied. "A condition where you wake up and don't know where anything's at, including yourself. But I'm sure my gun's in the drawer where I left it last night."

"Is there such a thing as awake confusion?" Howie asked. "But you're just in time for some blueberry pancakes at the Teewinot Cafe, courtesy of that famous chef, Sir Howard McPherson."

"How did you come up with pancakes without going to the grocery store?" Bud asked. "And I thought that only those knighted by the queen could be called *Sir*."

"That's only true if you're a Brit," Shorty said. "Here in the states, we can call anyone anything we want. That's why we had the Revolutionary War, you know."

Howie said, "There was pancake mix in the cupboard, but we're definitely going to need to get some groceries today, or the cafe's going to close."

"Is there any coffee?" Shorty asked.

"I brought some," Bud replied. "It's part of my survival kit. It's called Wicked Brew from a roaster up in Salt Lake. Wilma Jean gets it. But there's no cream."

"No vanilla ice-cream, either," Howie said. "No Shumway lattes."

Bud headed for the bedroom to get the coffee from his pack, and they were soon seated at the kitchen table, eating pancakes and drinking coffee, watching the moose as it casually grazed on the tall grasses and daisies in the yard, occasionally reaching to take a bite of aspen leaves from a nearby tree. Lindie was now begging under the table as Bud slipped her bites of pancake, the kibble he'd set out untouched.

"Are you sure the park's going to let us take Lindie in?" Bud asked.

Shorty replied, "I talked to Cam himself about it, Bud, and he said it was fine, since she's a search and rescue dog. She is certified, isn't she?"

"Not quite," Bud replied. "But she's such a good dog nobody would notice." He patted her head affectionately, slipping her another bite. "She's been pretty helpful before, and if nothing else, she can save us from things like wolves."

"Wolves?" Howie asked with concern. "Are there wolves in the park?"

"Howie, there are wolves everywhere up here," Shorty replied. "All over the place. There's a pack that hangs around Fred's Mountain, and another on Leigh Creek, both of which aren't far from here.

I actually thought I heard howling last night when I went outside, though it was distant."

"Is it dangerous to go out at night?" Howie asked.

"Wolves rarely attack people," Shorty replied. "Grizzlies are far more dangerous, and they don't usually attack people, either. And yes, there are grizzlies around. Don't forget, we're on the backside of a wild and rugged national park, part of what's called the GYE, or Greater Yellowstone Ecosystem. The top of the Grand Teton itself is only about 10 miles from here as the crow flies."

"I've read that moose actually injure more people than grizzlies and wolves combined," Bud noted.

Howie said, "Geez, in Green River all you have to worry about are gnats. Sometimes in the backcountry you'll see a rattler, but you have to go looking for them."

"Fellas, we may have something much more dangerous out here than the wildlife," Shorty replied. "And like I said, you can go home any time you feel uncomfortable, no honor lost. I signed up for this, and you didn't, as you came without knowing all the background details. But in a nutshell, here's what I know."

He paused to sip his coffee, then continued.

"Cam called me asking if I knew enough about fossils to help them out. I'm a geologist, not a paleontologist, but I am very familiar with a certain type of fossil, mostly because of my background with the Yukon Geologic Survey up in Canada. Cam knows about some work I did up there in British Columbia with what's called the Burgess Shale. So, I agreed to come up and take a look at what might be a similar fossil find."

Shorty stopped again, petting Lindie, who had now given up begging from Bud and was making the rounds, hoping someone else had leftovers.

He continued. "If it is another Burgess Shale type deposit, it's going to be really big in the paleontology world. But what's disturbing is the disappearance of the park geologist. He went up to check out this supposed find, and that's the last anyone's seen of him. Cam said a couple of hikers saw him on Teewinot, heard a strange boom, then he was gone. The sound may have been a coincidence, maybe not. So, even though we're dealing with trying to identify these fossils, there may be more going on than meets the eye."

"Like what?" Howie asked.

"It's possible that someone's already aware of them and selling them on the black market, someone who could be staking out their territory."

"Who first reported this find?" Bud asked.

"Apparently someone bought a fossil at a rock show in Cheyenne, and the seller said it came from the Tetons. Knowing it's illegal to collect from national parks, the buyer took it to the Park Service."

Howie asked, "Did they arrest the seller?"

"Cam said they tracked him down, and he said he'd gotten the fossil in Driggs, but didn't have any info on the guy he got it from."

"That's handy," Howie said. "Sounds like a dead end. But they really have no idea what happened to the park geologist? Will we be looking for him?"

"Not actively," Shorty replied. "But we'll certainly be keeping an eye out. The guy was also a law-enforcement ranger, which means he knew how to take care of himself. But Cam said they actually don't know the site of the fossil find, just the general area."

"So, what's on the agenda for today?" Bud asked.

Shorty replied, "You boys should probably get some good hiking boots, and also some groceries. I'll want you to take me over the pass and drop me off at the park headquarters, as I have a meeting with Cam, and I'll also pick up a park vehicle so we're not beating Bud's FJ to death. You can come on back here whenever you want, since I'll have my own ride at that point."

"Where do they think the area of the fossil site is, Shorty?" Bud asked, fiddling with his fork.

"I'm not familiar with the park, Bud, but Cam said they think from the geology it has to be somewhere around the head of Death Canyon, which opens up on the east side of the Tetons, but can also be reached from the west side. They got us this place here because it's way cheaper than Jackson, but it may actually be more accessible from this side, if we can figure out where it is."

"Death Canyon sounds like fun," Howie said. "Maureen's not going to like it if we die up here."

"I don't think any of us would like it much," Bud replied. "Anyway, I'm taking Lindie out for a minute, then hitting the shower. Let's get this show on the road."

"You're the only one not dressed, Sheriff," Howie reminded him. "Unless you're going out in those PJs. And watch out for that moose. Oh, and hang onto your jaw out there."

Bud looked puzzled, but Howie was already headed for his bedroom, so Bud opened the front door and checked to see if the moose was gone. Not seeing it, he walked Lindie around for a few minutes, wondering if he might die by moose, wolf, bear, or some unknown booming sound.

Now in a somber mood, he was questioning if he'd made the right decision by coming. He would know soon enough, he guessed, and like Shorty had told them, they could leave anytime they wanted.

He wanted to help his good friend, but he was already starting to feel somewhat outgunned by it all, especially since he wasn't sure where he'd left his Ruger, a first for him.

He hoped it was in the drawer where he thought he'd put it, his road weariness the previous night making everything a blur. Hopefully his confusion wouldn't be a portent of things to come.

Now around the back of the house and not seeing the moose, Bud took Lindie into a small grove of white-barked aspens. Looking through the trees, he instantly knew what Howie had meant about hanging onto his jaw, for there, in the near distance, stood the majestic and intimidating Grand Teton, towering above everything at nearly 14,000 feet, flanked on its left by Mount Owen and on its right by the Middle Teton.

All three peaks wore a cloak of white snow, their jagged spires reaching for a few wispy clouds scudding above them. He felt a sense of awe, yet also a sense of discomfort, for these mountains were the complete opposite of his home out in the boundless desert surrounding Green River where one could wander in relative safety, not likely to be killed by a predator or by falling from a cliff.

What he didn't know was that he would think of these big peaks for years to come, intrigued and yet intimidated by them at the same time, a feeling many experienced while gazing at their lofty summits, irresistibly drawn to their majestic danger.

3

As Bud's old FJ Toyota huffed its way up and over the steep ten-percent grade of Teton Pass, Bud wondered if Shorty might be getting them into things more complicated than he realized.

He suspected that Shorty had a higher opinion of Bud's detective skills than were warranted and hoped he hadn't oversold Bud's abilities.

He did know he didn't work well under pressure, as his methods for solving things were to take it slow and easy and let the facts reveal themselves, so he wasn't sure how things would shake out, especially since the house was only available for a few weeks. He'd decided to leave Lindie there for the day, as he had no idea what they would be doing, even though Cam had said she was welcome in the park.

They dropped down the east side of the pass, Bud gearing down the FJ to save his brakes. Even though he knew he was leading a parade, he wasn't about to go any faster, and there wasn't any place to pull over, so he just continued on down, slow and steady.

Once off the pass, the road straightened and he was finally able to pull over. A steady stream of vehicles passed, their drivers looking irritated. One guy actually shook his fist as he went by. Bud noted that the sign on his truck's door read:

Glided Tours!
Smooth as Silk!
Teton Gliding
Driggs, Idaho

"Wow, he must be in a big hurry," Howie remarked. "Probably going to get the typos on his sign fixed."

"I think maybe he has a glider, Howie," Shorty said.

Howie asked, "Wouldn't that be really dangerous, flying in these big peaks with all the up and down drafts? Especially without an engine?"

"Don't you have a birthday coming up?" Bud asked. "Maybe Shorty and I should pool our resources and buy you a glided trip."

Howie grimaced. "The only risks I like to take are in my songs."

"Your songs are risky?" Shorty asked.

"My songs are genre breakers. They cross that great divide between country and rock. Rockabilly."

"Wouldn't that be rock and hillbilly music?" Shorty asked.

"That's what they used to call country," Howie replied.

Bud said, "Howie, driving down this highway reminds me of that song you wrote about the highway of your love or however that goes."

Howie replied, "Oh, yeah, I remember that one well." He started singing:

I'm risking my life on the highway of your love,
A hundred miles an hour and it ain't fast enough.
With pedal to the metal on the throttle of your heart,
If my alternator falters I'll be needing a jumpstart.

"I see why they call you the Rockabilly Mayor of Green River," Shorty laughed.

"I think I make a better mayor than a deputy," Howie replied. "I mean, I remember when Bud first hired me on and he radioed me to do a welfare check on some old guy who lived in a trailer out by the ballfield because his daughter was worried about him. When I got there and roused him, he was pretty irate with me when I told him I needed to know if he'd gotten his welfare check yet. I thought everyone was just trying to help him out."

Bud laughed, then said, "You made a fine deputy, Howie, and I miss not having you around the office."

As they reached the edge of the small town of Wilson, Bud asked, "Where are we going, Shorty?"

Shorty replied, "The park headquarters are in Moose, but Cam's going to meet us at a place called Dornan's, on past Jackson and just before Moose. After that, you can go do whatever you want for the day, as I'm going back with Cam to his office to get all the details on everything, and I doubt I'll be back very soon."

The base of the Tetons were now to their left, the high peaks covered in wispy clouds that seemed to be dissipating as the air warmed up. Soon in the town of Jackson, Bud thought it was a bit overstocked with people, many looking to be outdoors-adventure types.

He saw one woman wearing a t-shirt with a bison butting a man into the air and the words, *Fly Yellowstone Airlines: Rough Takeoffs, Bumpy Landings*. Her partner wore one that read, *Free Bison Rides. Charges after the Ride is Over.*

Howie asked with concern, "Are there a lot of buffalo in the Tetons?"

Shorty replied, "Not in the mountains themselves. They're more over by Mormon Row and Gros Ventre areas, in the flats. But those shirts were probably bought in Yellowstone, where bison tend to gore people who get too close. A number of tourists have been put in the hospital, and a few even killed. Like moose, bison can be very dangerous."

"Is it buffalo or bison?" Bud asked.

"Either way," Shorty said. "Bison is technically correct, as they're not buffalo, but buffalo is the vernacular and what they were called historically, though the Sioux originally called them Tatanka. Bison means stinking animal."

"Maybe they gore people who call them bison instead of buffalo," Howie remarked. "I wouldn't blame them, knowing what it means."

Shorty replied, "I don't know, but buffalo as a word can also mean intimidate, and it's also a city in New York, as well as referring to buffalo meat. I read somewhere that you can use it to make the longest sentence in English with only one word: Buffalo buffalo Buffalo buffalo buffalo buffalo Buffalo buffalo."

Howie laughed, saying, "Translate."

"It means that someone from Buffalo buffalos or scares another person from Buffalo, who scares a buffalo, which scares another Buffalonian's buffalo—or something like that.

Howie replied, "OK, I get it. You know, Shorty, you could just keep going and make it the longest one-word sentence in the world, but nobody would understand it. You need to add stuff to the end of each word so people can figure it out—like Buffalonian and buffaloed and such."

Passing on through the town of Jackson, they continued north, and the grandeur of the Teton Range opened, the morning sun lighting the high peaks and making them glow. It was a stunning sight, one Bud had seen many years before when he and Wilma Jean had honeymooned there and in Yellowstone.

They were silent, taking it all in, and soon passed a sign that read *Grand Teton National Park*. As they passed the airport, Bud could see a private jet banking in front of the Grand Teton, getting ready to land at the only U.S. airport in a national park. He thought of how incredible it would be to take photos from a plane right smack in front of the Teton Glacier, with the big peak towering above.

It didn't take long to reach Dornan's, a large general store with a sign that read *Dornan's Pizza & Pasta Company*. It was a busy place, with cabins, a trading post and grocery, gas station, and equipment rentals. People were everywhere, but Bud finally found a place to park near a park-service pickup.

"What luck!" Shorty said as they all got out. "I think that's Cam's truck. Looks like him over there talking to someone. I haven't seen him for years, but he still looks the same."

He pointed to a thin man with dark hair in a gray and green ranger uniform holding a pizza box and talking to what appeared to be a couple of hikers with hiking sticks and packs. Cam saw Shorty and immediately came over, shaking his hand and whacking him on the back.

"You haven't changed a bit," Cam said. "And I assume this is Bud and Howie?"

Shaking their hands, he added, "Fellows, I really appreciate you coming up here, but things have changed a lot in the last few hours, so we won't be needing your services. Shorty, I ordered us a pizza to go so we don't have to wait. Bud and Howie, we'll catch up with you guys later."

He handed Howie a complimentary park pass along with a coupon for a free pizza, then turned to go.

"Hang on a sec. I need to get my jacket," Shorty said, grabbing it through the FJ's window. He turned back and said, "Cam, I know these guys are wondering what's changed, just like I am. I know I can brief them later, but if they're part of the team, shouldn't they know a little more now?"

Cam replied, "Of course. You're right, Shorty. It's just not something I was prepared to discuss right now, but I guess it doesn't really matter."

His manner became apologetic. "It was really nice meeting you two, but things have changed enough that we're not going to need your help. The house is rented for a few weeks, so you're more than welcome to stay. We're going to ask Shorty to help us with this fossil find, but that's pretty straightforward geology, and there's really nothing for you guys to do but enjoy the park. Let me know if there's anything I can do for you."

It was one of the few times Bud had ever seen Shorty speechless, and soon he and Cam drove away, leaving Bud and Howie somewhat perplexed.

"I think he should be a politician," Howie said. "He's good at answering the same question—not once, but twice—with a non-answer."

"Park supers are already kind of politicians," Bud replied. "They have to walk a fine line between government rules and answering to the American public."

"Bud, I have a feeling they found that geology ranger's body. Why else would they not need your detective skills any longer?"

"I'm thinking the same thing, Howie," Bud replied.

"But why didn't he just say that?" Howie asked.

"Maybe it's not supposed to be public knowledge yet," Bud replied.

The pair stood watching the tourists for awhile, then finally deciding to get a pizza, went inside, wondering if finding the ranger was indeed what had changed.

4

"That was kind of strange," Howie said as they sat at an outdoor table eating. "Cam asks Shorty to bring us with him, then decides not to include us after all."

"It gives us the chance to really enjoy ourselves," Bud replied. "We can do some serious sightseeing, yet maybe help Shorty in other ways."

"I can make dinner each night," Howie replied. "I'm a good cook. But since we're in the park, let's go drive around and see what we can see."

Bud said, "I wouldn't mind seeing Teewinot Mountain. For some reason, since we're staying in the Teewinot Cafe, it seems like a worthy destination. I wonder if anyone ever mistakes the old cafe for a real cafe and comes in looking for food."

"Maybe a bear or two, though I hope not while we're there," Howie replied. "But I think Teewinot Mountain is over by Jenny Lake."

They were soon back in Bud's FJ and at Moose Junction, where they stopped at the park entrance station and showed the pass to the ranger there, who wore a badge with the name *Jamie McKenzie*.

"Say," Bud asked. "How can we get to a good spot for viewing Teewinot?"

"Well, that's different," the ranger replied, handing them a map of the park. "Most people ask about the Grand Teton, which is pretty much visible from everywhere in the park. But if you want to get a good view of Teewinot, go to Lupine Meadows. You can see it in all its glory from there."

"Do many people climb it?" Howie asked.

"It's somewhat popular, but not as much as the Grand, even though it's maybe the most accessible of the peaks. Are you fellas thinking of climbing it?"

Bud and Howie both shook their heads no as the ranger continued. "The view from the summit is one of the finest in the range, with Mount Owen and the North Face of the Grand Teton directly to the southwest. Teewinot is Shoshone for *pinnacles*, and it's believed that the Shoshone used the term Teewinot for the whole Teton range. The summit is very exposed and big enough for only one person at a time. At 12,330 feet in elevation, it's the sixth tallest peak in the Tetons and claims more lives than any other."

"Why is that?" Howie asked.

Jamie replied, "Its difficulty is underestimated by climbers. Part of the climb is more exposed than many other routes in the park. Snow patches make an ice axe necessary. The down-climbing is what gets a lot of people—they get in trouble by going off route, as it's hard to navigate. Teewinot is the most dangerous in the Teton Range based on critical injuries and fatalities."

"You seem pretty familiar with it," Bud replied. "Have you climbed it?"

"Many times," Jamie replied. "I used to guide for Exum, and now I'm on the park's search and rescue team, and we go up it every so often."

"Exum's the climbing guide service here?" Bud asked.

"Yes, it's one of the guide services for climbing."

"And now you work for the park?" Howie asked.

Jamie looked thoughtful, then replied, "I got married and had a couple of kids. My wife convinced me they didn't want to be orphans, and she was right, so I switched jobs. I was an interpretive ranger for awhile, and helped man the booth, and sometimes I still fill in, but I'm actually a law-enforcement ranger now. But if you want to go a ways up Teewinot, assuming you're fit enough and comfortable with exposure, you should go. You can hike up to the Worshipper and Idol and call it a day, but keep in mind it's steep. Teewinot is one of the most beautiful places in the Tetons, and I would put climbing it in the top ten of my adventures."

"Thanks for the information," Bud said, noting a car pulling up behind them. "We're from Utah—just here for a short time. We're not much for climbing—we prefer moose and elk hunting." Bud held up his camera.

Jamie paused, and Bud noted his demeanor seemed to shift from friendly to serious as he said, "Hunting's not allowed in the park."

"I know," Bud offered. "I meant hunting with my camera."

"It's also illegal to carry a loaded gun in the park," Jamie added.

"I'm not armed," Bud replied. "But thanks for your time. We'll get out of the way of the people behind us."

As Bud began pulling away, Jamie asked, "Are you sure you fellas haven't been here before?"

Bud shook his head no, then drove on.

"That's kind of an odd thing to ask, don't you think, Sheriff?" Howie asked once they were on down the road.

Bud nodded in agreement, then added, "Howie, I wonder if he didn't have us confused with someone else."

Howie replied, "Man, he sure got hostile in a hurry."

"He acted like we were here to hunt the animals," Bud said. "I thought it was obvious I was talking about taking photos, but apparently not."

"You can tell he's a ranger," Howie finally said. "He sure knows a lot about the park. But Bud, I can't hike very far without getting some decent boots. There's no way I can hike up a mountain."

"Me, neither," Bud said. "But we can go a little ways, and if it gets too hard, we'll just turn around. It's going to be too late to get some boots today anyway. I can maybe get some good photos, but I'm definitely not into exposure."

"Bud, you have to be into exposure to take photos," Howie joked.

"Let's just go and enjoy the mountains," Bud replied, ignoring him. "This is pretty much a once in a lifetime opportunity for us. We'll stop when it gets too painful."

They continued on up the road, Bud wondering if they'd made the right decision to leave the peace and quiet of Green River to instead stumble around in the unknown dangers of one of America's most rugged mountain ranges, all the while not even knowing why they were there.

5

They reached Lupine Meadows, where Howie said, "We need to go another couple of miles down this gravel road, according to this map Jamie gave us."

"It sure is an amazing sight," Bud replied, nodding at the mountain towering over them, its numerous jagged spires making it look unclimbable.

They were soon at a small parking lot with several vehicles. Getting out of the FJ, Bud and Howie stood in awe for a moment, taking in the incredible alpine scene before them.

"I don't think this is going to be an easy hike," Howie remarked. "It looks pretty vertical to me."

Bud nodded in agreement, and they took off, immediately climbing up a steep slope scattered with huge boulders.

"These big rocks are what are called erratics," Howie informed Bud, looking again at the map. "They were carried on glaciers and then dropped wherever the glacier began melting."

It wasn't long before Bud stopped, huffing and puffing. His feet were already feeling the effect of the rocky climb, his heels rubbing against the heavy leather of his boots.

"These boots were made for riding around on tractors, not

hiking," he said to himself, trying to catch his breath. He could see that Howie was quite a ways ahead and would soon meet up with several climbers coming down the trail. As they all stopped to talk, Bud caught up.

"We made it to the top, but you guys don't want to try it without the right equipment," a man carrying a loop of rope over his shoulder and wearing gators was telling Howie. His two companions, a man and woman, carried small packs with ropes, ice axes, and climbing helmets.

A second climber said, "This was by far the hardest summit I've ever done. Lots of spots where if you fall it'll probably be your last. We heard a guy lost his life here last week. He was off route, which is very easy to do. It's really exposed, with lots of rockfall."

Bud thanked the climbers, assuring them they had no intention of climbing the peak, and as the group continued on down the trail, Howie said, "Sheriff, I don't want to quit yet. Let's go to that huge scree field just ahead."

"I think I'm starting to get some blisters, Howie. There's no honor lost in turning back. We're just not prepared."

"I'm going to try to get to that scree field," Howie said. "Then I'll reassess things. My feet hurt, but I have no idea if I'll ever be up here again, so I want to go as far as I can. You can wait if you want."

He then turned and headed up the trail, Bud reluctantly following. After many stops and much puffing, they eventually arrived at the small scree field, which was at the base of a steep cliff. A large gully they'd been skirting was on their left, partially hidden by trees and shrubs.

"This is it for me," Bud said. "I'm going to have some pretty serious blisters if I keep going."

"Me, too," Howie said, sitting on a large rock. "The view here's not bad. We can catch our breath. I bought some Snickers bars back at Dornans."

Bud sighed, found a large rock to sit on near Howie, and munched on a Snickers bar, then leaned back and closed his eyes. He had an unsettling feeling from the conversation with Jamie, which made him wonder if there wasn't more going on than met the eye, or if he and Howie were getting tired and just paranoid.

As he thought about taking off his boots to see how badly his heels were rubbed, he heard a muffled voice coming from the shrubs over by the gully. It was then he realized Howie was missing.

"Bud! Bud!"

Quickly on his feet, Bud rushed to where the voice came from. Pushing through what looked to be some kind of berry bushes, he saw Howie in a small clearing on the gully's edge.

"What are you doing over here?" Bud asked. "I didn't even notice you'd left."

"Nice to know you're looking out for me, Sheriff," Howie moaned. "I needed to take a whiz, so I came over here in the bushes. And lo and behold..." He pointed to a large shallow hole, dirt piled next to it.

"Somebody's been digging here, Sheriff," he stated the obvious.

They studied the hole, which was only a few feet deep but five or six feet wide. Bud could see boot prints in the disturbed dirt, which was a light gray color, just like the granite cliffs above.

Thinking of the missing ranger, Bud said, "Do you suppose this was some kind of grave, Howie?"

"If it was, it's barely deep enough. But Sheriff, it looks like someone dug it, then undug it."

"Undug? Is that a word?"

"Yeah, like they buried something, then dug it back up. I mean, look here on the edge where the dirt's still undisturbed, yet it's loose. See what I mean?"

"What's this?" Bud asked as he picked up a small clump of brown hair. "It looks like some kind of animal hair, like a deer. See how the hair's stiff and shiny?"

He took a napkin from his pocket and carefully wrapped the hair in it, putting it in his daypack.

"Maybe it's a buffalo wallow, Sheriff. Or do deer wallow? Do you think something bad happened here?"

"I don't know, Howie. I don't think deer wallow, and bison prob-ably wouldn't put in the effort to climb up here in the first place. But it definitely was dug by someone. We were told there's a ranger missing, but this doesn't look enough like a grave—like you said, it's not deep enough, and it's too wide. And who would bury anything way up here? Nobody in their right mind would drag or carry anything up that steep trail. It makes sense only if it was used to bury whoever was already here because this is where they died."

"Maybe they were digging for something, like fossils," Howie said, holding up a small gray rock. "Like this."

"Where did you find that?" Bud asked.

"It was in the hole. Just lying there, like someone lost it."

Bud examined it, saying, "It looks like some kind of strange millipede. Definitely a fossil, Howie, but it's illegal to take it with us, as this is a national park."

"I know that, Sheriff," Howie said, carefully placing it back in the dirt. "But what if it's something that would shine a light on what's going on here? Maybe I should keep it just in case. I bet someone dropped it."

"Howie..." Bud replied, now examining the tracks around the hole. "I have a feeling we should call a ranger about this. The whole thing just feels sketchy to me. These tracks are really distinctive. See how well-defined the little arrows are on the soles? And you can even make out the word *Vibram*. These look like fairly new boots."

"Take a photo, Bud," Howie advised.

"Good idea. But Howie, we're not part of the team anymore, not that we ever were. I mean, we're going to enjoy ourselves sightseeing, remember? Not investigating something that might not even need investigating."

Howie shook his head. "I don't know, Sheriff. It seems like investigating stuff is your destiny—and mine, too, at least when I'm around you. But you're right, the park superintendent definitely acted like he didn't want our help. Do you suppose he's worried that we'll figure out something that would implicate him or someone he knows? He did say things had changed in the past few hours. It makes me think they found the ranger, and this could be exactly where they found him, Bud, right here in this grave."

Bud, now taking photos, replied, "We're not really sure this is actually a grave, Howie."

"I know it's a grave, Bud, what else could it be? And wouldn't Jamie already know about this, being a law-enforcement ranger here?" Howie asked.

Placing his camera back in his pack, Bud looked at Howie with a steady gaze, saying, "Howie, I think you may be on to something. That would explain him asking if we'd been here before. I'm wondering if he doesn't think we might be involved in this, whatever it is."

"Like we were somehow involved in the murder of the ranger, Sheriff? How would that work? We just got here yesterday. We have alibis."

"But we don't actually know the ranger is dead, yet alone murdered, do we?"

"I wonder how the rangers ever found this grave in the first place," Howie mused. "Assuming they did."

"Probably with a drone," Bud replied. "But Howie, I need to get back and make sure Lindie's OK. I don't like the idea of leaving her in a strange place, especially as long as we've been gone."

"She's fine, Bud."

Bud now reached down and picked up the fossil Howie had left.

"Howie, I changed my mind about taking this. I think we should show it to Shorty. It may have some significance."

Now a voice from behind Bud said, "It's illegal to collect fossils, rocks, or anything else in national parks—we want to conserve the landscape for the next generation."

It was Jamie, and he had his hand on his gun.

Bud replied evenly, "Good to see you, Jamie. We were just wondering if you knew about this hole."

Jamie replied, "Criminals always return to the scene of the crime to make sure everything's like they left it."

"Was a crime committed here?" Bud asked. " Are you thinking we had something to do with this? We just got into town last night and can prove it."

"I need to see your IDs," Jamie answered.

As he and Howie handed Jamie their driver's licenses, Bud pointed at the grave and asked, "What happened here?"

Jamie replied, "You know more about it than I do."

Bud asked, "What kind of crimes did we supposedly commit?"

Jamie looked irritated. "For starters, discharging a firearm in a national park, transporting stolen material through a national park, disposing of a body in a national park, and theft of government property. I'm sure we can find a few more to tag on there before we're done, like that rock you're trying to pilfer. And we know whoever did this had Utah plates, just like you do—and they drove a 4 by 4 vehicle. It was dark when they came through the entrance station, but the camera recorded them. The light on their plates showed they were from Utah."

"So this is where the ranger's body was found?" Bud asked.

"I didn't say that," Jamie replied, looking both surprised and disturbed. "Put the rock back and start down the trail. I'll follow you."

Bud tossed the fossil back into the hole, then, shrugging his shoulders, said, "We were ready to go back, anyway. But your tracks indicate you've been here before."

He had just noticed that Jamie's tracks had well-defined arrows on the soles and the distinctive word *Vibram*.

"I was the one who found it," Jamie replied.

They started down the trail, Bud's toes now rubbing against his boots. He walked on, following Howie, wondering about the myriad crimes he and Howie had supposedly committed before they'd even arrived in the park.

He knew he should be more worried, but all he could muster right then and there was to worry about Lindie. For now, he just wanted to get back to the Teewinot Cafe and make sure his dog was OK.

6

Bud sat on the porch of the Teewinot Cafe, head in hands, feet sore, tired and discouraged, wishing he'd never come up north. If he was home, he'd instead be sitting on the porch of the bungalow playing ball with Lindie while Pierre and Hoppie hunted for rabbits in the back yard.

It would soon be dark, and Lindie was nowhere to be found. They'd come back late, having been questioned for some time by Jamie, who had finally decided he didn't have grounds for an arrest, something Bud had told him all along.

They had finally convinced him that there was no way they could've been involved in anything in the park, given they'd just arrived the evening before, and Bud could tell he'd seemed a bit disappointed upon finding out Bud was a sheriff.

When they finally got back to the house, Lindie was gone, apparently having let herself out the gate, which had a lever latch. She was smart, and Bud suspected she'd figured out how to push it up with her nose, probably having learned the trick from Shorty's dog Patches, who Shorty sometimes called Houdini Dog.

Bud didn't have a dog door at home, but Lindie had quickly

learned how to use the one here, and he'd left it open, worried about her needing to go outside if they were gone very long.

He'd walked all over the neighborhood when they'd gotten back, and Howie had driven it, all to no avail—no Lindie. It seemed odd, for she wasn't the kind of dog to wander.

His despair was an all-too-familiar feeling from when they'd rented a house on another vacation and Hoppie and Pierre, being the kind of dogs who *did* like to wander, had disappeared when he'd failed to properly close the door. He and his friend Doc had finally found them in a nearby grocery store's meat department, begging.

Thinking of Doc, Bud was now wishing he was here, for Doc's good-natured humor and jokes always cheered him up, and Doc was also good at coming up with ideas and solutions. Bud wondered if he could persuade Doc to come up and join them.

He jumped when his phone began ringing.

"Yell-ow," he answered.

"Are you missing a dog?" A woman's voice asked.

Bud replied, "Yes, I am. Do you have her?"

"Is her name Lindie?"

"It is!" Bud felt his heart pound as he pulled his FJ keys from his pocket. "Where are you? I'll be right there."

"I'm at 244 Packsaddle Lane. Good thing she has tags."

"I'm just down from the Teewinot Subdivision," Bud replied. "And I don't know the area. How do I get there?"

"Well, I guess you *don't* know the area," the woman replied. "Because it's just up the road. It's the buttercup yellow house with lots of white daisies in front. Look for a red convertible in the drive."

"I'll be right there," Bud replied. "And thanks a million for calling."

"You're quite welcome."

Bud opened the front door and yelled into the house that someone had found Lindie, and Howie was soon jumping into the FJ with him to go get her.

To his surprise, Packsaddle Lane was just around the corner, with the yellow house only a half-block away. He pulled up next to the red convertible, wondering how Lindie, who had managed to navigate a good deal of rough Yukon Territory on her own, had so easily gotten lost.

As he rang the doorbell, a tall dark-haired woman answered.

Bud introduced himself while Howie stayed in the FJ, and the woman invited him inside, telling him to wait in the foyer while she got the dog.

Bud could see into the living room, and it had high ceilings with tall windows that perfectly framed the Grand Teton. Someone must be a hunter, he mused, judging by the mounted heads of deer, pronghorn antelope, and elk on the walls, some trophy-sized with large racks. He quickly counted 10 points on one big elk.

She was soon back with Lindie, and noting Bud studying the heads, said, "My husband Mason is quite a hunter. But is this your dog?"

As Lindie jumped up like she had springs on her feet, happy to see Bud, the woman answered her own question.

"Well, I guess there's no question she's your dog," the woman laughed, handing Bud the leash. "I'm Jessica. I saw her in my yard earlier, and I figured she wasn't a stray, as her coat looks so beautiful and she's not thin, so I let her be, hoping she'd go home. When she didn't, I lured her inside with a pork-chop bone and found your number on her collar. She's been playing with Merriweather here." She nodded towards a small white fluffy dog inside the screen door that was wagging its tail.

"We've been looking for her all evening," Bud replied, relieved. "We're visiting and had to leave her for a bit, and she managed to open the gate. From now on, it gets wired shut."

"Or maybe just don't leave her alone in a new place," the woman said somewhat accusingly.

"We had to go into the park for awhile," Bud replied lamely.

"Well, anyway, welcome to the neighborhood."

Bud said, "Thanks, though we're just here for a couple of weeks, out seeing the sights."

She seemed disappointed. "You must be staying at that resort rental. I still don't understand how they can get away with that."

"Get away with what?" Bud asked.

"Having short-term tourist lodging next to an HOA-controlled subdivision. We would've never bought here had we known that we'd be dealing with tourists, no offense."

"I'm sorry," Bud replied, not sure what to say and now just wanting to flee. "We'll try to be good neighbors."

"Apart from letting your dog run," Jessica replied, watching an approaching truck. "Well, enjoy your stay. Looks like my husband, Mason, is home. Gotta go."

With that, she went back inside, leaving Bud amazed at how quickly she'd gone from being pleasant to hostile.

Lindie jumped into the FJ and Bud backed out just in time for a pickup to pull into the spot he'd just vacated, a sign on its door that read:

Glided Tours!
Smooth as Silk!
Teton Gliding
Driggs, Idaho

As the man got out, Howie said, "Bud, that's the same guy who shook his fist at you coming down the pass."

"I'm afraid so," Bud replied. "His wife's not so friendly either once she finds out you're a tourist."

"Ironic, as I bet they make their living off tourists if they do glider rides. But Sheriff, look at his pants and boots. They're covered with gray dust or something."

"Maybe he's been drywalling, Howie," Bud replied.

"Or digging a grave on the flanks of Teewinot. And he has Utah plates, Bud."

"We're not that far from Utah up here, so it doesn't seem that unusual," Bud replied, pulling into the drive.

"If he lives here, he should have Wyoming plates, Sheriff."

As they pulled up to the house, they could see Shorty on the front porch and a white pickup with a light bar on its roof parked in the drive. It had a green stripe and the National Park Service logo on the door, along with the words *Park Ranger*.

Shorty greeted them as they got out and gave Lindie a big hug.

"Are you a park ranger now?" Howie asked Shorty.

Shorty laughed, saying, "They could use a ranger with some common sense, if you ask me. That Jamie guy sure had you guys pegged wrong."

"How do you know about that?" Bud asked.

"Jamie came into Cam's office while I was there. He was pretty torqued that he had to let you guys go," Shorty replied. "Anyway, seeing how you guys didn't make it to the grocery store, it's a good thing I got us another pizza at Dornan's."

Howie groaned at the thought of more pizza, though Lindie's nose twitched at the smell of pepperoni.

They talked a little after dinner, but everyone was tired, and they soon went to their rooms. It had been a long day, and Bud was happy to finally crawl into bed, the curtains tightly pulled against the night.

Outside, lofty mountains and sparkly stars looked down as a curious moose grazed quietly under Bud's window, Lindie's nose twitching in her sleep.

7

"You could just say *buffalo* for the rest of your life, and you'd have the longest sentence in English using only one word—not just on Earth, but in the entire universe," Howie said, pushing a grocery cart while Bud tossed stuff into it. "Problem is, nobody would know what the hellsbells you were talking about."

"You'd obviously be talking about buffalos, Howie," Bud said. "Should we get some hot chocolate?"

"Sure," Howie replied. "Make sure it has marshmallows in it. But where does Shorty get such stuff?"

"Probably something he read while cruising through that black hole they call the Internet," Bud replied. "He's obviously not a linguist. Spaghetti?"

"Sure. Get the sauce with basil in it," Howie said. "He was telling me last night about some horseshoe-crab fossil they found where its brain was perfectly fossilized. He said it was over 300 million years old. Actually, let me get the ingredients and I'll make my own sauce."

"The one with the vodka in it?"

"Yes, though you can also use wine. The vodka makes the tomato base really creamy."

"It sounds pretty gourmet, Howie. We can run by the state liquor store, and I'll buy a bottle. I've heard rumors you make a really good marinara, and Shorty might drink the part you don't use—after all, he *is* a geologist."

Howie laughed. "Yeah, geologists do have that reputation, don't they, though I thought it was more with beer. But I make spaghetti sauce, not marinara, Bud."

"What's the difference?"

"Spaghetti sauce is richer and uses more ingredients than marinara, which is traditionally used as a dipping sauce," Howie said.

"Should we get some French bread to go with it?"

"Definitely."

Now in the bakery section, Howie carefully selected a loaf of French bread, then put a dozen glazed donuts in a sack, saying, "Since you can't go to the Chow Down while we're up here, these will have to do. But Bud, what did you think of all that stuff Shorty told us last night?"

Bud asked, "All what stuff? Seems to me he didn't really know much more than we did, except that the ranger is still missing. He had no idea what Cam meant when he said a lot had changed in the past few hours, because Cam never told him. And he has yet to see a fossil."

"I have a fossil right here he can have," Howie replied, pulling the one from Teewinot out of his pocket.

"I thought we left that," Bud said.

"I wanted to show it to Shorty," Howie replied. "So I grabbed it when Jamie wasn't looking. After all, aren't fossils the reason we're here? But I got the impression they found the ranger's body. Why else would Jamie suspect we had anything to do with that hole in the ground? And the charges he mentioned—discharging a firearm, disposing of a body—doesn't that sound like someone was killed to you?"

Bud replied, "Yes, it does, but apparently Cam said nothing about it to Shorty."

"Jamie mentioned Utah plates, Bud, remember?" Howie said. "He also mentioned something about a 4 by 4 vehicle. Seems to me he was just grabbing at straws to try to arrest us."

"You mean grasping at straws, Howie. But we don't even know if a crime has been committed. And Shorty basically said that it seemed to him that Cam had simply changed his mind about us helping, as he didn't ever give a reason."

Now at the meat department, Bud studied a sign above a small box while Howie selected some ground beef for the spaghetti sauce. Grinning, Bud quickly filled out a small form and dropped it into the box, making sure Howie didn't notice.

"I'm getting something for Lindie," Howie said, looking in the bargain meats bin, then putting a steak in the cart. "We need to treat her better so she won't run off again. Here's a nice porterhouse steak at half price. This store sure puts the Melon Harvest back home to shame. I guess Driggs must be a bigger town than Green River."

"It's only about 1500 people, according to the highway sign, but I think it serves a lot of people in the valley," Bud replied. "Including the 300 up the hill in Alta where we're staying."

They were soon checked out, and as they exited the store, an older woman with short gray hair stopped them. She was thin and wiry and wore brown cargo pants, along with a plaid cotton shirt and hiking boots, and from her tan looked to Bud like someone who spent a lot of time outdoors. She carried two full grocery bags.

"Excuse me, but is there any chance you could give me a jump? My rig won't start."

"Not a problem," Bud said. "Let us get rid of these groceries first."

The woman followed them to the FJ, and while Bud and Howie were putting the groceries in the back, the woman opened the side door and put her groceries onto the back seat next to Lindie, saying, "What a beautiful dog! What's your name, sweetheart?"

"Her name's Lindie," Bud replied, puzzled as to why the woman had put her groceries on the seat.

"You do have some jumper cables, right?" The woman asked, now scooting inside, her arm around Lindie's neck. "I loaned mine out and didn't get them back. That's why I'm in this pickle in the first place. My sister, Addy, which is short for Adeline, always told me I was too generous. I asked all over the campground, but no one had any, though one nice young man was able to give me a ride into town. I'm Winnie Meadows, and I really appreciate you helping me like this."

"You're welcome," Bud replied. "But where exactly is your rig?"

"Oh, it's up Teton Canyon. I'm the camp host."

"Teton Canyon? Where exactly is that?" Howie asked, getting into the front.

"You boys must be from out of town," she replied. "The canyon's up the road here a few miles, not far. It's a beautiful drive if you've never been up there, though the road's getting pretty washboarded. But I don't mind, as it keeps the tourists down. Lots of tourists these days—are you boys tourists?"

"Pretty much," Howie replied as Bud started the FJ. "I guess you'll have to give us directions."

"Just follow Ski Hill Road like you're going to the Ghee," Winnie replied. "You know, Targhee Ski Area. It splits and goes into Teton Canyon just before you start up Fred's Mountain. You'll enjoy the drive."

"We're staying just off Ski Hill Road," Howie replied. "Near Teewinot Subdivision."

"That's right on the way," she replied.

They were soon heading up the road, Bud wondering what they'd gotten themselves into.

"Howie, we need to stop by the house and put these groceries away before we go up the canyon," he said. "My ice cream will melt."

Stopping at the house, he and Howie grabbed the groceries, saying, "We'll be right back," leaving Lindie in the car with Winnie. But as they were putting the groceries away, Winnie appeared in the kitchen, Lindie behind her.

"I remember when this was a ski lodge, then a cafe. Times sure change. But you know, fellas, I'm not in any hurry. I bought some stuff for fish kabobs, and I noticed you have a nice grill on your deck. If I take these back to camp, it'll take me forever to cook them over a fire, so let's just barbecue it all up while we're here and have lunch."

"Don't you mean shish kabobs?" Bud asked. "And sure, that sounds like a plan. I could use some lunch."

"No, I mean fish kabobs," Winnie replied. "I have some nice tuna steaks, along with green peppers and squash. If you'll get the grill going and find some skewers, I'll do the rest."

Just then, Shorty came from the back of the house, looking puzzled at seeing a guest.

"Winnie stopped by to fix us lunch, Shorty," Howie said as he followed her out to the deck.

Before Bud could explain, Shorty said quietly, "Bud, I just got a call from Cam. They found the ranger's body, and it looks maybe like foul play. I think this was what had transpired to make him decide you and Howie shouldn't be involved, but he wanted to make sure from the autopsy before he told me."

"The ranger was murdered?" Bud asked.

"Nobody's saying, though he was hit in the head. They found him on Teewinot."

"Was it near where Howie and I hiked?"

"Jamie told me and Cam about that. He was sure off track suspecting you guys, but yes, the ranger was found not far from there."

"Does this make us suspects again?" Bud asked.

Shorty paused, then, as he could hear Howie and Winnie coming back inside, said softly, "No, you're clear, but someone with Utah plates was sighted in the area not long before they found the body—that's why Jamie suspected you."

"A body?" Winnie asked, having overheard. "I'm Winnie Meadows," she said, holding out her hand.

Shorty shook it, saying, "Shorty Doyle."

Winnie, looking at him with her direct green eyes, said, "I hear lots of rumors in the campground, one of which says developers are bribing the powers that be to lease a 500-acre site up Teton Canyon for ski area expansion. That's public land and butts right up to the park boundary. It's prime wildlife habitat, and I can't begin to tell you how much this has us locals up in arms, and there's been lots of infighting, especially between the oldtimers and the newcomers who have money and are skiers. And now it sounds like someone's maybe been killed over it. I hope it wasn't my friend Marty Langford, as he's been very vocal and has had some death threats."

She paused, then said, "That Park Service vehicle outside made me think of him, as he works for the park. It looks like you also work for the park. Are you new?"

"No, but I'm afraid it's not something I can talk about," Shorty replied.

"I'm just hoping it's not Marty," Winnie reiterated. "Well, come on out and help me make the kabobs and we can get to know each other a little better."

Shorty, looking puzzled, followed Winnie outside while Bud pondered how their simple grocery run had quickly transformed into a barbecue catered by a campground host who personally knew the victim of what appeared to be a murder.

8

Bud pulled his jacket up around him, the night's chill beginning to settle in as the campfire slowly burned itself into a glowing bed of coals.

It had been some time since he'd sat around a fire in the wilds, and he was enjoying himself immensely, though he was tired. Lindie's head rested on his foot as she dozed, and he knew they needed to head back to the Teewinot Cafe soon. He fished in his coat pocket for his harmonica, then realized he'd left it at home. He panicked for a minute, knowing he couldn't think without having something to fiddle with.

He and Howie had brought Winnie out to the Teton Canyon campground to jumpstart her old green VW bus and had soon gotten seriously sidetracked. Shorty had stayed home, saying he needed a break.

Howie had his hands cupped around a mug of hot chocolate, listening carefully to Winnie, who was talking so softly that Bud could barely make out what she was saying—something about having lived in her VW bus for a decade or more, moving to Utah in the winter to stay with her daughter and coming back to the Tetons in the summer. She also had a small canvas tent pitched in her campsite, which she said was her art studio, where she painted rocks with colorful mountain scenes to sell at art shows.

Bud moved closer to the fire, where he could hear the conversation better.

"I'm 71 years old, and I've been a road dog for many of those years, and I've loved every minute—well, with a few exceptions," she said. "When I'm not camp hosting or at my daughter's, I boondock in remote places with awesome views."

"Is it safe out alone like that?" Howie asked.

"I've never been bothered by anyone, but you may have noticed the sign on the door of my bus that says *Danger! Pitbull Inside* along with the photos in the side windows of a gnarly-looking pittie looking out. When anyone tries to scope me out from a distance they're not going to chance getting mauled. Don't get me wrong, I love pitties, and that's actually a photo of one my daughter has."

"Your dog photos win my Best Ever Self-Defense Tactic Award," Howie replied. "But do you actually have a dog?"

"Just the one in the photos—no need to feed or water it, no vet bills—none of that. I've always had dogs, but they always get old, then up and kick the bucket on me, and now I'm happy to just have Bijou."

"Who's Bijou?" Bud asked.

"Bijou's the body behind those two yellow eyes looking at you over on that rock. I bet you didn't even notice him, did you?" Winnie laughed. "Bijou's a gray tabby cat I got from the shelter in Driggs. He's actually more protective than a dog. He loves living like this—he's an adventure cat."

Winnie now gently pulled on a long lead, the cat at the other end coming to her.

"It's bedtime, Bijou," she said. "He goes outside, but only with his lead and harness, and when I'm outside, too. There's lots of coyotes out here who would just as soon eat him as go fishin'. They sing us to sleep every night, though I'm afraid to ask what the words to the songs are—probably something to do with filet de cat."

She continued. "My daughter worries about me, but there are

plenty of things you can do to increase your safety factor. For example, when you're out boondocking, always park facing your way out. It takes longer to park, but it's easy to get out in case of an emergency, like a fire or something. And I always think about when I was studying martial arts and the instructor told us to manage our distance from other people to stay safe, so I keep my circle small."

"Have you ever been in any danger?" Howie persisted. "I'm not sure I'd want my mom living like this. It seems dangerous."

Winnie laughed. "You're actually safer than in a town. If people can't find you, they can't harm you. And when I'm camp hosting like I am now, I have a radio I can call the rangers with, and the other campers tend to look out for me. I always make lots of friends."

Bud thought of how she'd jumped into his FJ, and as if reading his mind, she added, "I don't usually get into stranger's vehicles, but I had a good feeling about you boys, especially since you have Utah plates like my bus. But actually, about five years ago I was in a shootout. That's the worst thing that's ever happened to me. I was shot at first, and I never even got a shot back, as I got a direct hit. Don't ever tangle with a skunk."

She laughed, then continued. "But I read that most accidents happen within a 10 mile radius of one's home, so I move around a lot. And I'm always in bed before 2 a.m., as I once read that's when most crimes happen."

The cat started kneading her leg and purring as she added, "There's an old Guy Lombardo song that my mom used to sing."

Howie asked, "Who's Guy Lombardo?"

"He was a Canadian singer way back when, kind of in the big band era, back in the 1920s and 30s—Guy Lombardo and the Royal Canadians. The words go something like:

> You work and work for years and years, you're always
>   on the go,
> You never take a minute off, too busy makin' dough.
> Someday you say, you'll have your fun, when you're a
>   millionaire,

Imagine all the fun you'll have in your old rockin'
    chair.
Enjoy yourself, it's later than you think,
Enjoy yourself, while you're still in the pink.
The years go by, as quickly as a wink,
Enjoy yourself, it's later than you think."

Howie said, "That's kind of a depressing song. I prefer rockabilly music myself. And though I like to be in the woods like this, I like to go home at night. I had an RV once, but it got stolen, and I sold it after it was recovered. I guess I'm kind of a coward, 'cause camping doesn't feel very secure to me. It kind of intimidates me."

"Camping in bear country is a bit nerve wracking," Winnie replied. "This is grizzly country, and every so often we have to close down the campground because of bear activity. They come in and try to get people's food—black bears and grizzlies both. I always carry bear spray, but I've never needed it. Usually they run off. But if you boys do any hiking out here, you'd best carry it. We're very close to the national park boundary, and there's lots of grizz."

She paused to stroke Bijou's ears, then added, "But I know your Shorty friend isn't here for the scenery, since he's driving a Park Service truck, but I'll try to respect you not wanting to tell me anything about what you're doing, though if I knew I could help keep an eye out. I'm kind of information central out here. And I hear the ranger chatter on the radio."

"Would it be OK if I brought my telescope out here some night?" Howie asked, trying to change the subject. "This night sky is unbelievable."

"Sure," Winnie replied. "And I promise to quit asking about what you're doing. I guess it's really none of my business."

"Shorty's a geologist," Bud said measuredly, not sure how much to reveal yet wanting her to not be suspicious of them. "He's a friend of the park superintendent and is doing some kind of geology work for him. We pretty much just came along for the ride, and we actually know nothing about the body that was found, except it's a ranger, which we probably shouldn't even be mentioning, but I know you'll keep it to yourself. I'm sure it will be in the news once they decide to release the information."

"I just know it's Marty," Winnie worried. "He comes through here often but hasn't been around at all lately. He hikes a lot in the park. Like your friend Shorty, he's a geologist."

"You think someone may have killed him for his views on the ski-area development?" Bud asked. "People fight development all the time and don't get murdered for it."

Winnie stood and began kicking dirt onto what was left of the fire, holding Bijou close to her chest. Bud sensed she didn't want to talk about it, but she said, "Who knows? When money's involved, anything's fair game to some people. But I need to go to bed, boys. I've really enjoyed meeting you, and I appreciate the jumpstart. I know it's Marty, even though you don't want to tell me."

"The fish kabobs were really good," Howie said, he and Bud now putting out the fire.

"You bring your telescope out here anytime you want," Winnie said, now turning to go to her VW bus. She then turned back, as if remembering something.

"Marty and I were very close," she said sadly. "At one time, we were married. It didn't work out, and he got remarried and had a daughter, then divorced again, but we stayed friends."

She added, "He was a hard-rock miner before he got on with the Park Service. He has a geology degree from the Colorado School of Mines. He had a claim out in Nevada and sold everything he owned trying to make good on it. As far as I know, he still has it. He gave up on mining, couldn't make a go of it, and trained in law-enforcement and became an LEO ranger. He finally became the park geologist."

She paused, then added, "He filed a claim here by the park boundary, though he probably wouldn't want your Park Service friend to know, as the park might consider it a conflict of interest. When we were young and still married, we spent a lot of time in the park. We climbed almost every big peak in the Tetons, including the Grand several times. Climbing the Grand was an old tradition in his family going back several generations. We always wore helmets, as the Tetons have a lot of rubble. I still worried that some day one of us would get hit. Anyway, if you see him, tell him I'm worried sick about him. But my gut is telling me he's dead."

"Have a good night, Winnie," Bud said softly, getting into the FJ. He wanted to tell her it was indeed her friend, but he didn't know if Cam was ready for the public to know. Until then, he knew he couldn't say anything.

He added, "We'll see you again, I'm sure."

"You can count on it," she replied, opening the door to her VW bus and slipping inside, Bijou close at hand.

Bud saw a light come on, and he couldn't help but wonder if she was truly happy living like a nomad or if she had no choice and was trying to make the best of it.

Either way, he couldn't help but feel a hint of envy at her carefree life, and if the situation was ever right, he knew he'd like to give that lifestyle a shot.

He would rise with the sun, drink coffee and take photos, then come back to his rig and play with the dogs, fix lunch, take a nap, take the dogs for a walk, fix dinner, then wander around taking sunset and night-sky photos, moving every few days to a new landscape.

He shook his head at himself. It sounded good in theory, but he knew he was too much of a homebody to ever be a nomad. He could never survive without Wilma Jean's enchiladas, and how in hellsbells could he live without the luxury of vanilla-bean ice cream in his coffee?

As they drove down Ski Hill Road, Howie was quiet, looking out the window at the night sky, and Bud wondered if he was also thinking about being a wanderer.

Bud reached back and rubbed Lindie's head, then pulled up in front of the Teewinot Cafe, feeling bad knowing that the ranger had been found dead, but glad that Cam had decided that their help wouldn't be needed.

And as he later crawled into bed, tired and sore, Winnie's words lingered: *Enjoy yourself, it's later than you think.*

9

"This is quite the find," Shorty remarked, carefully examining the fossil Howie had picked up on Teewinot.

It was the next morning, and Howie had made them a breakfast of French toast with strawberries. They'd just finished and were drinking coffee when Howie had taken the fossil from his pocket.

Howie explained, "I found it in the grave and gave it to Bud, but the ranger made him put it back. I grabbed it when he wasn't looking. It just seemed out of place."

"That's because it was," Shorty replied. "This fossil looks exactly like an Hallucigenia."

"It does kind of make one think they're hallucinating," Howie replied.

"Hallucigenia is a fossil found in the Burgess Shale in Yoho National Park in British Columbia, Howie." Shorty replied. "It's a genus of Cambrian animal resembling a worm with long spines along its back. It also had teeth around its mouth but not *in* it, simple eyes, and another set of teeth *inside* its throat to aid in digestion. British paleontologist Simon Conway-Morris discovered it and called it Hallucigenia because of its bizarre and dream-like quality."

"How old is it?" Howie asked. "I mean, you said Cambrian, but how long ago was that?"

"Around 500 million years ago. It's the first geological period of the Paleozoic Era. But the mountain you found this on, Teewinot, is granite, not shale. The fossil's matrix is shale, so we know it was brought there by someone. Like I said, it *was* out of place."

"And what exactly is a matrix?" Bud asked.

"It's the rock around the fossilized remains of an organism," Shorty replied. "In other words, the type of rock the fossil is embedded in. Fossils are almost always found in sedimentary rocks like shale, not rocks like granite."

"Why?" Howie asked.

"Because granites are igneous or plutonic, which means they were altered by heat and pressure from their original state. It's part of what's called the rock cycle. Igneous rocks have zero fossils because they are completely melted and recrystallized. Shales are sedimentary until they're metamorphosed, then they become slates."

"Interesting," Bud said. "I wonder if it was left accidentally or if someone was trying to get rid of it in a hurry. If they were, there may be a chance they would return and look for it."

"If that's where they found the ranger's body, it could've been on him and fell off, Bud," Howie said. "Maybe he was in on the fossil looting."

"Or maybe he had it as evidence," Shorty said.

"I wish we knew if that was his grave or not," Bud said.

"Cam said he was found somewhere on Teewinot," Shorty replied. "But would someone actually bury him after killing him? Seems to me they'd be in a hurry to not be caught and would just hide his body in the bushes or something. Digging a grave takes a long time, plus you need a shovel."

"They didn't want his body found," Howie replied. "And I bet it *was* his grave. I mean, why would Jamie accuse us of killing him if it wasn't?"

"Howie," Bud said patiently. "I don't recall him actually accusing us of murder. Did he really say that?"

"Well," Howie replied, "He accused us of disposing of a body in a national park. What else could that mean? And discharging a firearm."

"But he also said transporting stolen material through a national park and theft of government property. How would that fit in?" Bud asked. "Shorty, was something stolen when the guy was killed?"

"I don't know, Bud," Shorty replied, now examining the fossil with his hand lens. "It probably had to do with the stolen fossils. But fellas, there's something wrong here. This fossil doesn't seem quite right."

"What do you mean?" Howie asked.

"There's something about the heft of it that's not right. I can't really explain it, but it's too light."

"Sandstone's not that heavy, is it?" Bud asked. "I mean, not like granite or something."

Shorty tossed the fossil to Bud, who held it in his hand for a moment, then handed it to Howie.

"It feels OK to me," Howie said. "But I'm not a geologist who knows rocks like you do, Shorty."

He handed the fossil back to Shorty, who stuck it in the sugar bowl on the table.

"Why put it in there?" Howie asked.

"I don't know," Shorty replied. "I don't want to carry it with me, as I might lose it, and it seems like a good place to hide it for now. But fellas, I need to get going. Cam and I are hiking up to where he thinks the fossil site might be, near Death Canyon. It's going to be a long day. What are you planning on doing?"

"I'm not sure, except I do know we're getting some new boots," Bud said. "And Howie's making spaghetti for dinner with vodka sauce, so we need to get some vodka. Other than that, maybe just do some local sightseeing, as I don't really feel like going anywhere much."

"Make plenty of spaghetti," Shorty smiled. "We're going to have some surprise company for dinner, so make enough for several extra people. If I'm late, save me some."

Bud groaned silently. He'd never been much of one for socializing and was hoping to spend a quiet evening on the back deck, playing ball with Lindie.

Howie was now searching through the cupboards.

"What are you looking for?" Shorty asked.

"Bingo!" Howie replied, holding up a crock pot. "I'm going to cook Lindie's steak so she can have a nice dinner with us."

"You're a lucky dog," Bud said, patting her head. "And you're going with us today. No more letting yourself out of the yard to run around."

Shorty was soon gone, and Bud and Howie headed into Driggs to look for hiking boots, Lindie in the back.

"Happy birthday, Howie," Bud said.

"Thanks. I kind of thought everyone forgot," Howie said somewhat mournfully. "I haven't heard a peep from Maureen"

"Howie, it's barely even nine in the morning. She probably hasn't had a chance to call you yet."

"You don't know my wife," Howie replied. "She's an early bird. I think she forgot."

"I'm sure she'll be calling you soon," Bud said. "But you don't mind cooking your own birthday dinner? I wonder who Shorty invited. We don't even know anyone up here, so I'm guessing it's someone from the park, maybe Cam."

"I don't think Shorty knows it's my birthday, so it's probably work related. But Sheriff, let's stop at this outdoors store here. It looks like they might have some boots."

"Wydaho Outdoors. That's kind of an odd name," Bud replied, pulling over.

"Probably because we're close to the Wyoming-Idaho state line," Howie replied.

As they walked into the shop, a short stocky woman with blonde hair was talking to a gray-haired man in neatly pressed cotton shirt and pants who looked like he would be happier on a golf course.

The woman said, "The difference between us and everywhere else is that we're surrounded by potatoes, and potatoes don't ski."

"And the Ghee gets 500 inches of powder a year," the gray-haired man replied. "That's why this development is going to be such a good thing for the valley. All that snow is begging to be shared."

The woman replied, "You're going to ruin everything that makes this place special, Parker, which is partly the lack of people. Some of us here prefer to keep it that way."

"But Georgie, think of the business you'll get," Parker answered. "You West Siders don't appreciate how much you're all going to benefit from this. You'll be thanking me with bouquets of roses for years to come."

"Look," the woman said heatedly. "We don't want luxury hotels, Persian rug galleries, or year-round Christmas stores. We can go to Jackson for all that, though we prefer not. We have everything we need and want here. Who else has a drive-in theater with a huge potato parked out front? We want people who can help you frame your house or help plow your drive. We have no desire to sell out to big money. And to be honest, I'd prefer to not see you in my store again."

Parker turned to go, then stopped, and upon seeing Bud and Howie, said in a low voice, "Fine, Georgie, but you know somebody's going to come uncorked, and then there will be hell to pay. Let's try to keep it civil."

"That sounds like a threat. Are you aware Marty Langford has been killed?"

Parker turned white as Georgie added, "Get out!" and half pushed him out the door, then, looking somewhat embarrassed, turned to Bud and Howie, saying, "I apologize. That's Parker Watson, the guy who wants to expand the Ghee, and the whole valley's against it. He has some nerve to come in here and try to talk me into it. But what can I help you fellas with?"

"Are tourists OK in here?" Howie asked nervously.

"You're fine," Georgie replied. "As long as you're not here trying to make money off us."

"No, we're here to *give* you our money," Bud said. "We need some good hiking boots."

"Go over there and I'll fix you up with the best," Georgie said, pointing to the boot section of the store. She then quietly added, "You fellas are lucky. Sometimes I wish I was just a visiting tourist and knew nothing about the dang politics here. But let's get you some boots."

10

"Those look really nice on you," Georgie said, admiring the pair of new boots Howie was trying out, walking around the store. "Teton Lites are very popular with the rangers here and typically last about 1,100 miles, which is about one summer."

"These are really comfortable," Howie said. "But I need something that lasts longer than one summer."

Georgie added, "If you walk over a thousand miles each summer, you're not going to find much of anything that won't wear out. But I'm talking about backcountry rangers. Do you walk that much?"

"I try not to walk at all," Howie replied. "I usually ride around in my wife's VW Bug, and Bud here, he doesn't even walk, unless he has no choice, but instead rolls around his equipment shed in his old office chair. We both get lots of exercise just pushing our luck."

Georgie laughed, then added, "Make sure to moisturize the leather."

"On my office chair?" Bud laughed.

"No, the boots, silly," laughed Georgie.

"How much are they?" Howie asked.

"$350, which is actually a good deal, as they're on sale. Twenty-percent off."

Howie was speechless, so Bud tried to help him out by saying, "It's your birthday, Howie, get yourself a nice gift. They'll last you forever."

Howie said nothing, sitting down next to where Bud tried on an identical pair of boots.

Georgie turned to Bud and continued, "These boots really are top quality. You can't go wrong."

"They *are* comfortable," Bud said.

"Hand me your old boots and I'll put them in the boxes."

Bud felt a little pressured, yet they needed boots, and he knew there wouldn't be much of anywhere else to get them in a town the size of Driggs. They would probably cost even more over in Jackson.

"That's more than my monthly allowance," Howie moaned.

"You get an allowance?" Georgie laughed. "For real?"

"My wife gives me one," Howie replied. "But I usually end up spending it on diapers."

Georgie now eyed him with suspicion.

"He has a toddler," Bud said.

"Oh, of course," Georgie laughed.

"Today's his birthday," Bud added.

"Oh my gosh!" Georgie laughed. "I'm going to throw in a birthday gift—a carabiner with a little turtle light on it."

She took a tiny plastic turtle attached to a carabiner from a display and handed it to Howie, who nodded his head in thanks, looking puzzled.

After they paid and were walking out the door in their new boots, Bud remarked, "Howie, I think she thought today was Malcolm's birthday, not yours."

"Really?" Howie asked. "I thought it was kind of a strange gift, but that would make more sense. It's kind of cute. I'll give it to him when I get home."

He clipped the carabiner onto his jacket as they got into the FJ, Lindie happy to see them.

"Let's go get a bottle of vodka," Howie said.

"Where's the liquor store?"

"We'll go straight to the source, Sheriff. Go on past the airport to the Grand Teton Vodka Distillery. I saw their ad in a brochure back at the house. They make potato vodka."

"Seems appropriate for Idaho," Bud commented. "Does this mean our spaghetti is going to taste like spuds?"

"I hope not," Howie replied. "The ad said they make it from Idaho potatoes and pure glacier water from the Tetons, then filter it through charcoal and garnet crystal."

"Sounds expensive," Bud said. "How will you know if it's good or not? Taste it first?"

"I would guess so," Howie said. "Though I really don't know much about what a good vodka tastes like—or a bad one, for that matter."

They soon turned off the highway and parked in front of a modern-looking building with a small tower that was reminiscent of the Grand Teton behind it in the distance. Inside, they were greeted by a man who said the tour and tasting didn't start for an hour, but they were welcome to browse the gift shop.

Bud picked up a bottle under a small sign that read, *Gluten-Free American-Made Craft Potato Vodka*. Next to it was a graceful pink bottle that reminded him of Old Man Green's Watermelon Spritzer sold in the Melon Harvest Grocery back in Green River.

"Look, Howie, Grand Teton Huckleberry Vodka. It says it has real mountain huckleberries, and since huckleberries can't be cultivated, it says they go off the beaten path to have them picked."

"I'm going to buy a bottle, Bud. It'll give a new dimension to my cooking—authentic Teton spaghetti."

"Look at this cute dog scarf," Bud said. "It says Teton Distillery under a neat sketch of the Tetons with dog paw prints. I'm going to get it for Lindie. And look at this dog toy—it's a plastic Vodka bottle."

"Lindie would love that."

"I'm going to buy it, though Wilma Jean would probably worry what people would think if it looked like the dogs had taken up drinking."

Howie, now on the other side of the store, said, "Look, Sheriff. We can buy a high-efficiency stainless-steel still for only $23,000. It makes 158 gallons at a time."

"Might be a nice gift for Old Man Green," Bud said. "But let's get out of here. This is too much like shopping, and it's making me nervous."

They paid for their stuff, and as they walked out the door, Howie said, "Sheriff, I don't want to sound like a worrywart, but Maureen still hasn't called me. It's not like her, especially on my birthday."

"Why not just call her?" Bud asked.

"Good idea."

Bud waited as Howie dialed the number, but no one answered.

"Now I *am* getting worried," Howie said. "Do you think it would be out of hand to have someone do a welfare check?"

"Well, no, but who would you have do it? The sheriff's missing in action."

"The mayor wouldn't work, either," Howie replied. "Maybe I could call the Melon Rind and see if someone there would run over to the house real quick. It's not far."

"Might work," Bud replied. "I know Wilma Jean would do it if she's there. Let's drive over to the fairgrounds and let Lindie out for a bit while you call."

Bud was soon playing ball in a grassy field with Lindie while Howie paced back and forth, then finally came over and said, "Nobody's answering at the Melon Rind. Do you suppose something happened to Green River after we left? Have you talked to Wilma Jean lately?"

"Actually, not since I called to tell her we got here OK. But what are you thinking, that the entire town was abducted by aliens or something?"

Bud dialed Wilma Jean.

"Hi, hon, what's up?" She answered.

"Howie's trying to get ahold of Maureen and she's not answering. Is there any chance you could run over and check on things?"

She laughed. "No need to worry. She's right here with me."

Bud sighed in relief. "Good. Everything OK? What's that humming noise in the background?"

"Humming noise? I don't hear anything. Must be a bad connection."

Howie was now tugging on Bud's sleeve, and Bud asked, "Howie wants to know how little Malcolm is doing."

"He's fine. His grandparents are visiting and he's having a ball."

"Oh, good. I'll let him know."

"I'm going to lose you, hon, We're coming into a canyon."

"A canyon? Are you on the road somewhere?" Bud asked, but it was too late, as the connection had dropped.

Putting his phone back into his pocket, he said, "Howie, all's well. I was going to have her put Maureen on the phone to wish you a happy birthday, but the signal dropped. It sounded like they were going somewhere."

"Probably shopping in Grand Junction or Price," Howie replied. "Hopefully getting me a belated birthday present."

"I don't know how they can find any fun in shopping," Bud replied. "But say, let's go have a birthday lunch—I'll buy. Then we can go find me a new jacket somewhere and maybe get something to take back to Maureen and Wilma Jean."

"Sounds good," Howie said, though Bud could tell he was disappointed to not talk to his wife.

"We'll see them all before you know it," he added, trying to make Howie feel better.

"I'm not getting any younger, Sheriff, and I miss my family," Howie said somewhat morosely. "I'm not made for running around without them."

"Well, wherever you go through life, just remember to always side with yourself, and you'll be OK," Bud said, patting him on the shoulder. He then tied the Teton Distillery bandanna around Lindie's neck, just as his phone rang.

"Yell-ow," he answered.

After listening for a moment, he said, "Just a minute," and handed Howie the phone, saying, "It's for you."

Surprised, Howie answered, then after pausing, said, "I actually don't recall entering a contest."

Bud whispered, "I entered it for you."

"Oh, OK, I guess I did enter it, and you're saying I won? What exactly did I win?"

Howie listened, then said, "I'll be there right away."

Howie, looking slightly dazed, said, "It was the grocery store. I just won a free glider ride."

"Congratulations," Bud replied. "A new pair of boots, a turtle light, a free lunch, and now a glider ride—your birthday seems to be looking up."

Howie grinned, then handed Bud a small wrapped present. "I got you something, Sheriff, since you left your harmonica behind, and I know you can't think without fiddling. Besides, it's not fair that I get all the presents, just because it's my birthday."

Opening it, Bud laughed.

"A yoyo with *Teton Distillery* on it. Thanks, Howie."

"I might want to borrow it once in awhile," Howie added.

"Any time," Bud said, dangling it off its string. "Let's see if I can remember how to do Around the World."

"I can show you some tricks, Bud, like Walking the Dog, the Elevator, and Rock the Baby."

"I didn't know you were a yoyo pro," Bud replied. "But let's go get your prize at the grocery store."

"OK, but I'm not sure I want it," Howie said. "I dunno about flying around without a motor. It reminds me of a joke about a fellow who took off in a hang glider one day and flew above his hillbilly ma and pa's house out in the country."

"Go on," Bud said.

"Well, Pa had never seen a hang glider, and he yelled for Ma to run and get his shotgun, thinking it was some kind of giant bird. He shot at the hang glider, but it kept going. Ma said, 'You missed,' and Pa replied, 'Yeah, but at least it let Johnny go.'"

Bud groaned, then, putting the yoyo in his pocket and getting Lindie back into the FJ, said, "Let's go, Howie. I'm sure you'll enjoy the glider ride."

With that, they were soon headed back into town.

11

Bud sat in a swing on the back porch of the Teewinot Cafe, playing with his new yoyo while throwing the ball for Lindie. The sun was starting to set, alpenglow slowly lighting the flanks of the Tetons in a ruby light, a few bright gold fluffy clouds hanging above the Grand Teton itself.

He thought about getting his camera, but he knew by the time he got it and put his telephoto lens on, the light would have faded. Besides, he was enjoying just kicking back, admiring his new boots and how comfortable and secure they made his feet feel.

He'd never owned a quality pair of hiking boots, always wearing his Wolverine work boots, and he knew Howie felt the same with his new boots, as he always wore his old Carhart Wellingtons, neither brand really made for hiking.

Who knows, maybe the two of them would become famous hikers, starting with the Appalachian and Pacific Crest trails and eventually working their way up to hiking across entire continents and such, boot companies paying them to use their names for marketing, fans following them across mountains and prairies, wanting them to autograph their boots.

Thinking of mountains, he wondered how Shorty's day had gone hiking up Death Canyon, looking for the fossil site. It was almost dark, so he hoped he would be back soon, and besides, Howie's spaghetti was almost ready.

Bud had gone inside not long before to check on things, where Howie was stirring the sauce, which instead of being a nice creamy tomato-red color, was a kind of sickly-looking purple. Somewhat defensively, Howie had said, "It tastes really good, in spite of how it looks, Bud, so don't be put off."

"What's in it?" Bud had asked.

"Tomatoes, huckleberry vodka, heavy cream, butter, parmesan cheese, and fresh herbs. The vodka adds a touch of heat to help balance out the sweetness of the tomatoes and the cream. The huckleberries add something I can't quite describe. Here, have a taste."

Bud conceded it was delicious, though he, too, would be hard-put to describe it. He then took off back to the porch before Howie could conscript him into helping out, as he wasn't much of a cook, though he would be happy to set the table when the time came.

He knew Howie was getting more and more depressed about not hearing from Maureen, and Bud hoped she would call soon. If not, he might just call Wilma Jean and ask her to put a bug in Maureen's ear. It wasn't at all like her, as she seemed to be pretty conscientious about such things.

Now Bud began wondering again about the ranger's death and the fossil that Shorty had said didn't quite feel right. It had felt OK to him, but he wasn't a geologist, though he did have to concede that its appearance would give one nightmares, if it still existed. Of course, that would depend on how big it got—as it was, it seemed more like a centipede or such.

It was now dark, and he was beginning to wonder when Shorty would be back when he heard a vehicle drive up. Lindie was now on full alert, and she soon began whining. He heard a car door slam, and thinking it was Shorty, let her go. She quickly disappeared around the front of the house.

Bud stood, but before he knew it, he was almost knocked off his feet by something small that had quickly attached itself to his pant-leg, growling. He instinctively tried to shake it off, but it was now joined by another something, this one jumping up and down, trying to grab his hand. Now Lindie was there, tail wagging, and someone had turned on the back porch light, and Bud was able to see what was attacking him.

It was Pierre and Hoppie, his wiener dog and Bassett hound! What in hellsbells were they doing here, he wondered, petting them and tousling their ears as they whined.

Now Wilma Jean was hugging him, and soon Doc and Millie were there, too, laughing.

"Surprise!" His wife said. "We decided it wasn't fair for you guys to have all the fun, so we closed everything down and headed out early this morning. Maureen's here, too. Her parents are taking care of Malcolm. We wanted to surprise Howie for his birthday."

"How did you know where to find us?" Bud asked, still in shock.

"Oh, Shorty's in on it. Where is he, anyway?"

"He should be back any minute," Bud said as they all went into the house. "But he said not to wait for him for dinner. I imagine you guys are tired and hungry. Let's unload your stuff and eat. Howie's making gourmet spaghetti."

"It smells delicious," Maureen said.

"That's Lindie's crockpot steak you smell," Howie replied. "Now she can share it with her little buddies."

After dinner, they all sang Happy Birthday to Howie, and Maureen brought out a cake she'd made, then a present.

"You're going to love this, sweetie," she said to Howie, who unwrapped it to find a t-shirt with a picture of a planet on it and the words, *Pluto, May We Never Forget, 1930-2006.*

Howie immediately put it on over the long-sleeved shirt he was wearing, then turned to Bud and Doc, saying, "For you non-astronomy types, Pluto was discovered in 1930, but lost its planetary designation in 2006."

"I kind of remember reading about that," Doc said. "What does it take to be a planet these days?"

Howie, now in his element, answered, "It has to orbit the sun, be massive enough to be rounded by its own gravity, and has to have cleared the neighborhood around its orbit."

"Cleared the neighborhood? What does that mean?" Maureen asked.

"It means it's gravitationally strongest so there aren't any other bodies in its orbit. But Pluto was eventually found to be part of a belt with some objects larger than it, so they kicked it out of the planetary club."

Doc asked, "So it's forgotten but not gone?"

Howie groaned, then said, "By the way, I brought my telescope, so if anyone wants to look at the stars, I'll set it up on the back deck."

Bud now began picking up the dishes and cleaning up while everyone else went into the living room. Howie had gone from being morose to talking non-stop about everything they'd seen and done so far, telling them about Winnie and the distillery and climbing partway up Teewinot and his new boots, as well as how he'd won a glider ride, which he was scheduled to take the next morning.

Now thinking of the distillery, Bud remembered he'd bought the dog toy shaped like a vodka bottle, and as he went to get it, it dawned on him that the dogs hadn't been hanging around the table, begging for scraps, like they usually did.

He quickly ran into the bedroom, thinking maybe they were tired from the trip and were sleeping, but no dogs.

"Hon, have you seen the dogs?" He asked Wilma Jean as he hurried to the back porch. He hoped they were outside enjoying the yard after the long car ride, but a quick search revealed nothing.

Now everyone was searching the house, and Doc had gone out the front, looking, even though it was dark.

Bud stood at the front door, watching as Doc walked up and down the street, calling, and a sense of foreboding hit like a freight train—a train carrying despair and a sense of irresponsibility with it. Beyond the small subdivision, all there was were miles and miles of wilderness—wilderness with wolves and bears and mountain lions and all kinds of things that could prove fatal to pampered domestic pooches.

He'd been so distracted by everything that he'd not only left the dogs in the back yard, but left them for some time, at least an hour or so, and though the gate had been closed, he hadn't wired it shut, though he knew Lindie could open it. They could be anywhere by now, especially with Lindie leading them astray, for, like Bud, she enjoyed seeing new places and new things.

And now that it was getting late, where was Shorty? Even though he'd told Bud not to wait dinner for him, surely he hadn't intended to be back this late.

As he turned to go back inside, his phone rang.

"Yell-ow," he answered.

"So much for being a good neighbor," a woman's voice said accusingly. "Your dog's back, and it's got a whole pack with it this time. Come and get all of them or I'm going to call the sheriff."

It was the neighbor, Jessica.

"I'll be right over," Bud said.

"You'd better hurry," she replied. "They're scaring my little Merriweather to death. My husband's about ready to have a fit."

Bud suspected she was the one about to have a fit, but all he said was, "I'm on my way," and headed out the door.

12
―――――――

It was nearly midnight, and Bud was stretched out on the couch, trying to get some rest, unable to sleep, wondering where Shorty was. Everyone else was fast asleep, and he'd promised Howie he'd give him a ride to the airport in the morning, so he was hoping Shorty would come back soon.

Bud had gone to bed earlier, but had gotten up, paced a little, and was now on the couch, Lindie sleeping on the floor next to him, the boys in the bedroom with Wilma Jean.

It had been a hectic evening, with the birthday dinner and then settling everyone in, and he'd been especially stressed by the dogs getting out, but Jessica had been almost pleasant when he'd described what had happened. Of course, taking her a couple of slices of the delicious cake Maureen had made had helped, the element of surprise kind of taking some of the wind out of Jessica's sails.

He was glad the gang had showed up, and he thought back to when he'd wished Doc was there, having no idea his wish would come true so quickly. There was something about him that helped Bud deal with things better, maybe Doc's sense of humor.

As if on cue, Doc slipped into the living room, wearing his pajamas, and sat down in a leather recliner near Bud.

He whispered, "No Shorty yet, eh?"

Bud sat up, Lindie taking the opportunity to jump up on the couch next to him.

"Not yet," he replied in a quiet voice. "I'm sure he's fine, but he said he and the park superintendent were going to hike up to look for some fossil site. It doesn't seem right that he wouldn't at least call."

"Maybe there's no cell service in the park," Doc replied.

"I don't think there is, Doc, but surely he's back to Jackson by now where he could call. But I figured that since he was with the park super, Cam, things would go well. No chance of him getting lost or anything like that, not that Shorty would. After spending so much time in the Yukon, he's pretty adept in the back woods."

"Can you call Cam?" Doc asked.

"I tried his office number, but no answer, and I don't have his cell number."

"Well, about all you can do is sit tight. Even if he's out all night, he'll be OK. It's not getting that cold or anything."

"True, unless you're way up in the mountains, which they were going to be. It's probably pretty chilly up at 10,000 feet. And the fact that the park geologist was killed doesn't help matters any."

"Do you have any theories as to what might be going on?" Doc asked.

Bud shook his head no as Lindie, maybe sensing his distress, snuggled closer. "Shorty seemed to think something was off with the fossil Howie found. Maybe it was faked somehow, though I have no idea how one could fake a fossil. I'm wondering if someone didn't make up the story that there's a big find up in the Tetons and then were selling these fake fossils on that premise."

"Do you think they're trying to stage the place the fossils came from?"

"I think that may be the case. If they could produce photos or even take people in there, it would be much more convincing. But it's also illegal to take anything from a national park, so I'm wondering if this so-called find isn't just outside the park boundary or something, though Cam seemed to think it's actually inside the park."

"And someone was murdered?"

Bud sighed. "The park geologist appears to have been killed by a blow to the head. I guess it could be accidental, but probably not."

"Have you seen any evidence of anything illegal?"

"I'm not in on the actual facts, Doc, but Howie and I found a grave that could have been his. The park ranger there with us tried to accuse us of killing him, so it makes me think he was indeed murdered."

Doc, now tapping his fingers on the chair's arm, obviously trying to think things through, asked, "Why in hellsbells would he think you and Howie had anything to do with it?"

Bud pulled the yoyo from his PJ pocket, and handing it to Doc, said, "Here, use this. It'll help you figure it all out for me. I have no idea why he suspected us, except apparently whoever did it had Utah plates."

"Lots of people have Utah plates," Doc replied, now fiddling with the yoyo. "An entire state full of people, actually."

He tossed the yoyo back to Bud, adding, "Nice try on getting me to start fiddling like you do."

Bud laughed, then said, "That reminds me, I found some hair in the grave. Since you used to be a coroner, maybe you can make some sense of it. It's in my jacket pocket."

"Stay put, Bud. I'll get it. We don't want to wake the sleeping princess."

Lindie was now stretched across Bud's lap, sleeping soundly.

Picking up Bud's coat, Doc said, "Nice jacket! It looks brand new."

"Yeah, Howie and I did some shopping today. We got a little carried away, as it was his birthday."

Doc laughed, now looking through Bud's jacket pocket. "Let's see, you've only had it since today, and you've already accumulated a napkin from some place called the Teton Diner, a receipt from the same place, a pen that also says the Teton Diner on it, two quarters, and a squeezable plastic liquor bottle."

"So that's where I left it!" Bud replied. "Toss it over here."

Doc tossed the bottle to Bud, who deftly caught it, not waking Lindie, then added, "And here's a napkin with what looks to be hair folded in it."

Doc sat back down, examining it.

"Elk hair."

"Not human?"

"No, too course and stiff. Definitely elk. I've seen lots of elk hair. This is from the grave you found?"

"It was on the edge of the grave."

"Not real definitive then," Doc replied.

"Probably not. Some elk walked by and shed some hair. No mystery there," Bud said, then asked, "Doc, what spurred you guys into coming up here? Was Wilma Jean worried about me?"

"No, Shorty called and invited us to come up. I guess you had some special assignment with him that didn't pan out, so he felt it would be a good thing for the rest of us to join you."

"Yeah, the park super asked if I would help Shorty with this assignment, whatever it is, then changed his mind. But I'm now thinking that maybe Shorty wanted you guys up here so Howie and I would stay longer."

"Why would Shorty care, if he's gone all day and apparently also all night?"

"I don't know, Doc. I just have a hunch he's into something deeper than he signed up for, and I think he's aware of it, too. That's partly why I'm so worried about him not coming home."

Just then, Millie poked her head around the corner of the hallway.

"Everything OK?" She asked.

Doc stood. "Shorty's not back, but that's no reason for us all to be sleep deprived. I'm going back to bed. Bud, let me know if there's anything I can do. You might as well go to bed, too."

"Might as well," Bud said. "As soon as Lindie decides to let me, nodding as the dog chewed the toy. "She's on the bottle right now."

Doc laughed, then he and Millie went to bed, leaving Bud to wonder if Shorty was really in some kind of danger or just having a long day in Death Canyon. He hoped it was the latter, or maybe just shooting the breeze with Cam over a beer or two in Jackson.

13

"See, here in the Tetons," Howie explained, "One can soar only from late morning to early afternoon, about three hours each day, as that's when the cumulus clouds gather and provide good thermals. After that, the rain showers spread and the lift is gone."

Bud, driving Howie to the airport, asked, "How do you know this?"

"I read it on the website for the glider company. That's why, unlike when you do a balloon ride, it's better to wait for mid-morning to go up."

"I'm glad, Howie, as it let me sleep in a little, but I'm still pretty tired."

"What time did Shorty come in?"

"I'm not sure. I went to bed around two, so it was after that. The dogs woke me, but I didn't think to look at the clock."

"I bet he's tired. I wonder why he was so late."

"I'm sure he'll tell us later when we get back. How long will you be gliding, anyway?"

"I think it's about an hour-long ride."

"How gliders fly is a mystery to me. What keeps them up in the air?" Bud asked.

"They're full of potential," Howie replied. "They convert potential energy to kinetic energy, transfer altitude into velocity. They get lifted on a thermal then come back down. But I'm not so sure I want to do this, Sheriff."

"You'll be fine, Howie. Think of it this way, how many people get to fly over the Tetons in complete silence? Do you have your camera?"

"I do, but do you really think we'll be going over the mountains?"

"Sure, that's where you get the updraft to give you that potential energy you mentioned."

"Can I borrow your yoyo to fiddle with?" Howie asked, sounding nervous.

Bud laughed, turning into the drive for the airport and pulling over next to an office with a sign that read *Teton Gliders*.

"Say, Howie, do you mind if I just let you out? I think that guy Mason might recognize me, and if so, his wife probably has him thinking I'm some kind of pest. Call me when you're done. I'm going to take the dogs over to the fairgrounds."

Bud was soon throwing the ball for Lindie while Pierre and Hoppie sniffed around in the big field by the rodeo grounds. It wasn't long before a plane pulling a glider took off from the nearby airport, and he could see it climb and climb until it was high in the sky, then release the glider, which immediately banked toward the Tetons.

Bud suddenly felt a sense of trepidation. What if something bad happened? He began feeling guilty for instigating the ride by entering the contest on Howie's behalf, who hadn't really even wanted to go up.

Lindie had now abandoned the ball in favor of helping the other two dogs enlarge a nearby hole, the home of some kind of rodent, probably a gopher, Bud figured, making them stop.

He searched the sky, hoping to see the glider, though it was long gone. He could see the first wisps of clouds forming high above the Grand Teton.

Absentmindedly pulling the yoyo from his pocket, he began fiddling with it—up, down, up, down. Howie had researched yoyos a bit after giving it to Bud and said that the name came from Tagalog and meant *come and go.*

Trying to see if he could do an Around the World, he noticed the dogs again digging at the gopher hole, so he gathered them up into the FJ. He would drive into town and get a coffee at the espresso drive-through and maybe he'd run into the gang. He knew they'd gone shopping.

Just as he was ready to pull out onto the highway, his phone rang.

"Yell-ow," he answered, seeing it was Shorty from his caller ID.

"Morning, Bud. Are you in the vicinity?"

"I'm at the fairgrounds. What's up?"

"Just calling to see where you are, since everyone's gone," Shorty replied. "Any plans for lunch?"

Bud replied, "I'm just killing time until Howie gets back from his glider ride, and everyone else is shopping."

"Howie's taking a glider ride? That's a surprise."

"He won it in a contest," Bud replied. "I'm on my way to get a coffee. We're all wondering why you were back so late."

"I got involved in a SAR incident. I'll tell you about it when we get together."

"Come out to the fairgrounds, and I'll meet you with a coffee and cinnamon roll. I hope the search and rescue incident turned out OK," Bud replied.

"It mostly did," Shorty said.

Bud was soon back at the fairgrounds with coffee and rolls, where Shorty waited in the ranger pickup, looking tired.

"Glad you made it back," Bud said, handing him a cup of coffee. "So, what happened?"

"Well, everything was going just fine yesterday until it wasn't," Shorty said, sipping the hot drink. "Cam and I hiked up Death Canyon looking for the fossil site, though we didn't have any luck. It's a pretty good hike up there, and the scenery's incredible, so I guess there's that."

Sounding frustrated, he continued. "Cam had gotten some waypoints from the park geologist's GPS, and we followed them, but when we got up to the Death Canyon barn and patrol cabin, he heard on his radio that a party was in distress. They were clear over on the Grand Teton, so there wasn't anything we could do, and we'd decided to keep going, but once we got to the intersection with the Alaska Basin Trail, Cam got another call. Because of the scope of it all, he decided we needed to head over that way. We hiked the four miles back to his truck and drove over to Lupine Meadows, where the SAR team was assembling, along with a chopper."

"What do you mean by the scope of things?" Bud asked, now looking to the sky, hoping Howie would be back soon.

"It was a party of four, Bud. One was knocked off the edge of the wall they were on and was dangling upside-down by a rope. They were on the edge getting ready to rappel down when it happened, and it was a good thing the one guy was already roped in or he wouldn't have survived. The other two were suffering from what appeared to be various contusions and shock. It took a group effort to get them all off before dark, but it got done. Cam and I both helped get them off the chopper and into ambulances there at Lupine Meadows. The guy dangling upside-down was barely alive and seriously injured, but it looked like he was going to make it."

"Sounds pretty intense. What caused the accident?"

Shorty leaned back, saying, "Look, isn't that a glider coming in? I bet that's Howie."

Gathering the dogs into the FJ, Bud said, "I need to go pick him up. You want to meet us back at the house?"

"You guys go ahead with your plans, 'cause I need to go take a nap," Shorty replied. "But Bud, Cam thought the incident had the possible markings of a lightning strike—they were knocked off their feet and were bruised, yet it doesn't quite add up."

Bud shook his head. "I've read that lightning can strike some 15 miles from the storm."

Shorty, getting into his pickup, said, "The skies were clear from horizon to horizon, nary a cloud. I know, because I'm very aware of lightning from my time as a field geologist. I always keep an eye on the sky."

Starting the truck, he added, "Cam and I talked extensively with the ones who were well enough to talk, and they said they heard a loud boom before they were hit—nothing at all like lightning, and there was no thunder."

"That's what the people who saw the ranger before he died said, too, isn't it?"

"Exactly," Shorty replied tersely. "It's kind of strange, but I think it may have been a small earthquake. This is one of the most seismic areas on the North American continent."

As he began backing up he added, "I'll see you back at the house."

14

Bud and Howie sat in the FJ near the banks of the Teton River at Bates Bridge, one of several put-ins and take-outs for people floating the river, as well as for fishermen. It was only a few miles west of Driggs, and they'd come there to eat their lunch of sandwiches from the grocery store, the rest of the gang nowhere to be found.

"Was it as scary as I imagine it would be?" Bud asked, tossing bites of his sandwich to the dogs in the back. A half-dozen vehicles were parked along the banks of the small river, and a lone fisherman was out in the middle in his waders, casting in the slow waters.

"It was something I'll never forget, Sheriff," Howie replied. "I wasn't sure I wanted to go up, but it was actually an amazing experience, though I'm not sure I would do it again—actually, I'm sure I'll never do it again. I was scared half to death." He paused, then asked, "Sheriff, what happens if you're scared half to death twice? Are you dead?"

Bud laughed, then replied, "No, you'd still have a quarter of a life left. The first time you go from one to one-half, so the second time would be half that, which is one-fourth. But did you go up over the Grand and Teewinot and all that? Could you see any climbers? Were they like tiny little dots?"

"We were close, but not right over the top," Howie replied. "We went up to 17,000 feet, and I had to put on this oxygen thing. Apparently the glider pilot doesn't normally go that high."

"Was it that guy Mason? And why did he take you up so high? It seems like you might not want to risk your clients' lungs like that."

"It was Mason, and I don't think he really meant to, Bud. It was an accident. He was actually thrilled about it, though I was scared to death when I realized what was happening. See, we got caught in what he called a dust devil, though there wasn't any dust, it was more like a high-powered vortex. He called it an express elevator. We started going in a big circle, climbing and climbing so fast it seemed like the glider wings might fall off. I was terrified until I saw how much he was enjoying it, so I decided to try to figure out what was so much fun about it, but I didn't have much luck. When we got to 15,000 feet, he said that we needed oxygen, and he told me how to put on this mask thing. He then tried to break free from the thermal, but it still took us up another 2,000 feet."

"I've never heard of such a thing," Bud replied. "A dust devil way up at that altitude?"

"It forms when a warmer body of air breaks loose from the ground. The air rushing in to replace it begins a counter clockwise rotation, and once you're in it, right turns allow you to core the thermal, as he put it. But at 20,000 feet, you have 10 minutes without oxygen until you're unconscious. The plane has oxygen systems with automatic flow rates that vary by altitude, but he said he's never had to use them with a client, as he never goes that high."

"Gosh, Howie, I feel kind of guilty for getting you into all that."

"No, don't feel that way, it was the experience of a lifetime and very exciting. We were climbing at 1,500 feet per minute. He said that most climb rates for a glider are between 400 and 600 feet per minute, and most single-engine airplanes have trouble climbing at 200 to 300 feet per minute at that altitude."

"I hope you got lots of photos," Bud replied, watching a blue heron wade along the river bank. "That bird's sure tame," he added.

"I can't wait to look at my pictures when we get back. But Bud, I think I know where the fossil site is that Shorty's looking for. Mason made a beeline for this area kind of south of the Grand Teton, saying he wanted to check something out. He flew over what he said was the head of Darby Canyon, and finally got up pretty high above these big peaks, and I could see the Grand and all that, then he kind of dropped over this big saddle and skimmed the top of a small mountain."

"He sounds kind of reckless, Howie."

"Maybe, but I think he just knows the mountains really well and where to find the thermals. But we got down really low to where we could see a couple of people, and it looked like they were digging in the lower flank of the mountain."

"Did you get any photos of them?"

"Yes."

Bud asked, "Do you think these people were digging for fossils?"

"I don't know, but they were digging for something. There were two of them. They were kind of up in the layers of a small cliff, but we flew over them so quickly that it was hard to see much. We can check out the photos when we get back to the house."

"Were they in the actual park itself?" Bud asked.

"I don't know. It kind of looked like it to me, and if not, they were close. We can check it out on a map. But Bud, there was also this..."

Howie dug deep in his jacket pocket, taking out something about an inch long and handing it to Bud, saying, "Sheriff, I think it's another one of those fossils."

"Man, you should've been a paleontologist, the way you find this stuff," Bud remarked.

"It was on the floor of the glider," Howie said. "There was a small box that Mason pushed under the seat when I got in, and I think it came from that."

Bud, now holding the fossil up, replied, "This is almost as weird as that Hallucigenia thing. Not quite, but almost."

"I want to show it to Shorty. Where is he, anyway?"

"He went home to take a nap. We might as well go on back. The gang should be getting home soon, then we can decide what to do for the rest of the afternoon."

As they sat there, finishing their lunch, a green VW bus pulled up at the other end of the parking area, next to the river. Bud and Howie watched as a woman got out, slipped a daypack onto her back, then carefully made her way to the riverbank. Bud knew she hadn't noticed them, as the FJ was angled away from her.

"It's Winnie!" Howie whispered. "And she hasn't seen us. I wonder what she's doing."

After slipping a bit in the mud and nearly falling, she recovered, then startled as the blue heron lifted into the air over her. The fisherman had gone on down the river.

Bud could hear voices coming from up the river, and Winnie, seemingly panicked, quickly took off the pack. Swinging it toward the water for momentum, she threw it, and it made a splash and quickly sank. As two inflatable kayaks rounded the bend toward her, she turned, got into the bus, and drove off.

"That was odd," Bud said.

"Everything about this trip so far has been odd, Sheriff," Howie replied, nodding in agreement.

"And here comes another something odd, Howie," Bud replied. "It's the gang, whooping it up and having a blast, all without us. They must've rented some boats."

"So that's where they went," Howie replied. "But Sheriff, I have a bad feeling about that pack Winnie threw into the river. Do you think maybe we should try to retrieve it?"

"We have no idea how deep the water is there, Howie. It was probably just something like old letters from her past or such. Besides, it's kind of none of our business."

"It was too heavy to be letters, Bud. And that fisherman was there earlier in his waders—it can't be too deep."

The gang was now steering their boats to shore, laughing and splashing water on each other.

"How did you know to meet us here?" Wilma Jean asked with surprise, her kayak bumping against the bank. "The shuttle driver said to call him when we take out, and he'll come pick us up. We were going to take out at Rainey, but we had a moose come after us, and now we're kind of nervous."

Helping pull Doc and Millie's kayak to shore, Howie said, "We need your help to get something out of the water."

Doc asked, "Did you drop something?"

"Kind of," Howie replied. "Though it was someone else who actually dropped it. Doc, help me out. Wade out with me—you're already wet. Hold onto me while I look for it."

Howie and Doc were soon out in the water, which was only knee-deep, Howie poking around with his feet, trying to find the pack while Doc held onto him.

"It's probably already on down the river, Howie," Bud advised. "Be careful!"

Just then, Howie reached down into the water, getting soaked, but coming back up with the pack.

"Voila!"

Lugging the soaked pack back to shore, he opened it, looked inside, then said, "It's a rock. Nothing but a big rock. Man, am I ever gullible. Probably some kind of practical joke."

Bud hoisted the dripping pack into the back of the FJ, saying, "You and Doc can dry off while we wait for the shuttle, then let's all go back to the Teewinot Cafe and kick back for awhile. After all, it's not every day one gets to see a rock saved from a watery grave in the river."

Howie groaned, then went to help Maureen and Wilma Jean deflate their kayak.

15

"I made pretty good friends with a tree once," Howie said. "It was a good listener, but I've never been much of one to befriend rocks, unlike Shorty, here."

"Well, Howie," Doc replied. "As the painter Bob Ross once said, there's nothing wrong with having a tree as a friend."

Howie, Bud, Doc, and Shorty sat on the porch of the Teewinot Cafe, looking at the damp pack that Howie had retrieved from the river.

"We might as well take the rock out, Howie," Bud said. "Maybe Shorty, as a geologist, can figure out why someone would throw it in the river."

Howie opened the pack, but as he pulled out the supposed rock, they could see it was actually a large rectangular metal object.

"It's not a rock after all," he exclaimed. "It's some kind of plaque, though it's pretty beat up. It looks like bronze." He rubbed it with the sleeve of his jacket. "What does it say? Can anybody read it?"

Doc got close to it and began reading:

COMMEMORATING
FIRST ASCENT OF THE GRAND TETON, AUG. 11, 1898

BY THE PIONEERS HON. WILLIAM O. OWEN, ENGINEER AND
SURVEYOR REV. FRANKLIN S. SPALDING, FRANK L. PETERSON
AND JOHN SHIVE, RANCHERS
THIS TABLET PLACED HERE DURING THE CONVENTION OF
THE NATIONAL EDITORIAL ASSOCIATION HELD IN JACKSON
HOLE IN CONNECTION WITH THE DEDICATION OF THE
GRAND TETON NATIONAL PARK
JULY 29, 1929
BY THE DIRECTION OF THE STATE LEGISLATURE OF
WYOMING (S.J.R. NO. 3, 1929) BY E.M. FRYXELL, PHIL SMITH,
WILLIAM GILMAN
THE TABLET IS THE GIFT OF EMMA MATILDA OWEN

"Wow," Howie said. "If this is the real deal, it's pretty historic. But why would Winnie throw it in the river? And why did she have it in the first place?"

"Good questions," Doc replied. "And I have more—who's Winnie? And how did you guys know we were on the river?"

"Winnie's the camp host in Teton Canyon," Bud replied. "And we had no idea you were on the river—it was just a coincidence. But do you fellas think this was stolen? It seems to me like something one would see in the town square in Jackson, or maybe even in the national park itself."

"Agree, probably at one of the pullovers where you can see the Grand Teton," Shorty said. "And it seems to me it was stolen, the way she was trying to get rid of it. Dumping something in the river is a good indication you don't want to be seen with it."

"Or want anyone else to have it," Doc added. "What should we do with it?"

"It would probably be a good idea for Shorty to take it to Cam, since he's the park superintendent," Bud said. "He probably knows all about it."

"Maybe," Howie replied. "But how would something made of brass get so beat-up? It's warped and looks like it's been hit by lightning."

"Bingo!" Bud said. "If it was placed at the top of the Grand, it would be a prime lightning attractant, and that would account for how it looks. It must weigh 20 pounds and would be kind of hard to haul up there, but it could be done."

"The name William O. Owen is familiar," Shorty said. "I bet he's the guy they named Mt. Owen after. And if I recall correctly, the Owen Spalding Route is one of the main routes for climbing the Grand, along with the Upper Exum Ridge. Cam was telling me all about climbing it."

"It should be called the Owen Spalding Peterson Shive Route," Howie remarked. "Just to be fair."

"That would add five pounds to the plaque, Howie," Doc said. "But why would someone want to steal it?"

"Maybe they replaced it with a newer one, though that still wouldn't explain why Winnie would throw it in the river," Bud said.

"I don't know," Howie replied. "It doesn't seem right to toss something this historic. There has to be something behind it all."

"I'll ask Cam about it when I see him," Shorty said. "But Howie, Bud said you found another fossil. Can I see it?"

Howie dug the fossil from his jacket pocket and handed it to Shorty, who studied it carefully, then finally said, "This looks like an Opabinia *regalis*. It's another Burgess Shale fossil, and like Hallucigenia, it's one of the most famous fossils in the world. Its five eyes and long flexible proboscis tipped with spines were thought to be a joke when it was first presented at a scientific meeting in 1972, and scientists were shocked to find out it was the real deal, with its segmented trunk and flaps along the sides and fan-shaped tail. It's thought to have lived in the soft sediment of a seabed, using its proboscis to dig into sand burrows after worms. It was generally around three inches long, and its proboscis was an inch long."

"How old is it?" Doc asked.

"It's from the Middle Cambrian, around 500 million years—that's half a billion years."

They all sat in silence, trying to fathom deep time, until, finally,

Howie said, "Do you think this one is for real? I mean, you weren't sure about the Hallucigenia one."

Shorty examined the fossil with his hand lens, then bit into it, saying, "Something's off with this one, too. Fossils are encased in sedimentary rock, and when you bite into it or whack it with a rock hammer, you always get a few bits of rock spalling off, but this is totally intact. It just doesn't seem right, but I can't figure it out. I'd like to send it to a lab. I have a contact down at the University of Utah who could look at it under a microscope and run some tests to figure out what it is."

"So you think it's fake?" Bud asked.

"I'm not sure, Bud, but I want to show it to Cam and get his permission to send it off. Do you have any idea where it came from? We aren't having any luck at all finding that supposed fossil site."

"That's because it isn't in the park, Shorty," Howie said. "You don't need Cam's permission."

Shorty, looking surprised, asked, "You know where it came from?"

"Maybe," Howie said. "I have some photos I took, and maybe we can figure it out from them. But if it's where I think it is, it might be out of the park boundary. Bud and I were going to check it out, but we haven't had time."

"And Shorty," Bud added, "Maybe we would be wise not to mention this to Cam. Let's send it off and wait to get the results first. If it was on public lands, it's legal for us to have it, since it's not a vertebrate fossil—am I right?"

Shorty, looking perturbed, asked, "You're thinking Cam might be in on something illegal? Like stealing fossils? Why would he do that, then ask us to come up here and help him figure it out?"

"And then ask us to back off, remember?" Bud replied. "I'm not saying Cam is in on it, Shorty, and these aren't illegal if not in the park, though I bet a lot of paleontologists would like to know about them. And we know Marty Langford's death could be related to all this. It's just a hunch, but we just need to be careful, that's all."

Shorty nodded his head in agreement, pocketed the fossil, then stood, saying, "You know, fellas, geology is like being a detective at a crime scene. Just like you, Bud, when you're trying to solve a mystery, we geologists have to look at the scene and the evidence before us and try to come up with a cohesive story explaining it all. These fossils are a mystery, and so far, at this point, given all that's happened, the clues seem pretty sparse."

He stood, adding, "Let's go inside and look at those photos. I have a feeling we might be doing some hiking tomorrow, if we can figure out where that site actually is. I'll have to give Cam a rain check instead of going over to Moose."

Howie groaned. "If it's where I think it is, it's going to be one long hike. We'll be putting our new boots to a real test, not to mention our feet and knees and everything else."

Shorty, looking at his worn boots, added, "I need some new boots, too. And I just hope that, wherever this fossil site ends up being, it's not a one-way trip."

16

Bud, Howie, Doc, and Shorty were in the kitchen of the Teewinot Cafe, studying the photos from Howie's camera, which Shorty had downloaded onto his laptop.

Maureen, Wilma Jean, and Millie were outside on the deck drinking coffee and plotting their day's activities, which included a possible trip to Jackson to go to the National Museum of Wildlife Art, as well as to the Pendleton Store.

Bud was all for the first activity, but felt a sense of futility about the second, as he figured it would involve spending a goodly sum of cash, though he knew he couldn't say much after buying an expensive jacket and new boots.

"Are you with us here, Bud?" Howie was asking, bringing Bud back to the task at hand as Shorty said, "You got some good overview shots, Howie. I think we can figure out where these are."

He opened a second window on the laptop, brought up Google Earth, then zoomed in on the area around the Grand Teton.

Howie explained, "We flew towards the Grand, then banked to the south, and that's when we got caught in that express elevator. Man, we were up high, and I got a good look at the entire range from

17,000 feet. The pilot, that Mason guy, finally broke free and we glided back down a few thousand feet and to the west of the Grand. Mason said he wanted to check something out, so we gradually lost enough elevation that we weren't far above the mountains. At that point, I was worried we were going down too fast, kind of the opposite of the express elevator."

"That's where these were taken, then, right?" Shorty asked, pointing to a photo that showed an overview of a mass of peaks and spires. "This looks like the top of Teewinot."

"We didn't actually crest over the Tetons to the east side, but we almost did," Howie replied.

Shorty, now looking at the computer, asked, "Where exactly did you turn to come back around to the Driggs Airport?"

"We came out right there," Howie said, pointing to the screen. "See that big drainage? We followed that back out of the mountains and then turned toward the airport."

"That's Darby Canyon," Shorty replied, "Let's go back to your photos and see if we can coordinate them to the exact spot where you saw the two people digging."

He now toggled back and forth between the two views, pulling up different photos as he tried to follow the path of the glider.

Watching intently from the side, Doc said, "There! That's it. See how that mountain has that long ridge? That's the one right above the figures in that photo."

Shorty zoomed in, saying, "You're right, Doc. It matches exactly. You can even make out this same huge boulder. It's a good landmark —looks like an erratic."

"As in a boulder brought in by an ice sheet and dropped in place as the ice melted?" Doc asked.

"Exactly," Shorty replied. "The Tetons are highly glaciated."

He toggled back to a photo with two tiny figures at the foot of the mountain.

"It looks like they're digging, but if I zoom in any farther, it gets too pixelated to tell anything."

Now switching back to the Google Earth window, he said, "Well, that's ironic as heck. It says it's Fossil Mountain."

"Seems appropriate," Doc replied.

"And Mason seemed to be real interested in those people," Howie said. "He went way too low. They looked up at us and he waggled his wings, which sacred me to death. I'm never going up in one of those contraptions again, that's for sure."

Bud said, "Howie, I'm sorry I got you into that."

"No, no, Sheriff, I actually really enjoyed it—well, afterwards, when I was positive I wasn't going to die up there."

"Howie, technically, you wouldn't die up there, you'd die down here," Doc said, pointing to the floor.

"I kind of don't like mountains very much," Howie replied. "I'm more of a desert kind of guy. The ground isn't meant to go up like that. It's unnatural."

Shorty, now scanning the landscape, said, "It looks like you can get up there pretty easily by hiking up Darby Canyon. I know there's a cave at the head of the canyon that's a popular local hike."

He zoomed in closer and said, "See this big hole in the cliff band here? I think that's the cave. And down here, in the wash, see this big black rock? It's called the Black Bread Rock—apparently it looks like a loaf of bread. It's another erratic."

"How far do you think it is to Fossil Mountain?" Bud asked.

Shorty paused, then answered, "I scale it at somewhere around five or six miles from the Darby Canyon trailhead, one-way, with lots of elevation gain, but not too bad. But it also looks like you could hike down Teton Canyon to get back, though it looks farther and maybe trickier. Darby Canyon looks like the best route up, as it's not as steep."

"Is Fossil Mountain in the park?" Doc asked.

Shorty looked closely at the map, then said, "No. This line's the boundary. It's close, but not quite. And it's really not that far from the head of Death Canyon on the east side, so Cam and I weren't too far off."

"Death Canyon looks like the long way up there to me," Bud said, taking the yoyo from his pocket. "But fellas, this looks like something we need to prepare for, I mean, with plenty of food and water and gear. And we need to get an early start. I propose we wait until tomorrow and spend today getting ready, then head up Darby Canyon before dawn."

Doc added, "And that will of course give you more time to learn yoyo tricks. But if the gals are all going over to Jackson today, we'll need to dogsit anyway. They can watch the dogs tomorrow."

"I can take Lindie with us tomorrow, but you're right, Doc. No more leaving little bad dogs alone. Want to see me do Walkin' the Dog?"

Shorty laughed, then added, "That would mean I can go see Cam today, as planned. I'm not sure what he has going, but hopefully not another hike up Death Canyon."

"Are you going to tell him we think we know where the fossil site is?" Bud asked.

Now scanning through the remainder of Howie's photos, Shorty replied, "I'm pretty sure he'll want to go with us. After all, that's why I came up here, was to help him out. Howie, you have some really nice shots here, but what's this one? An accident?"

Howie studied the photo, then said, "No, I took it intentionally. It's a shot of the box on the floor of the glider. I guess I thought it might be some kind of a clue after I found the fossil. Zoom in on it."

The photo showed a small box with the words:

PRIMA
CREATOR
Value
DLP Resin
Brown

"Resin?" Bud asked. "Why would he have a box of resin?"

"It's probably recycled and has something else in it," Doc said.

Bud stood looking at the photo for some time, then said quietly, "Howie, I think it is indeed a clue—a very big clue."

He was silent for a moment, then added, "Let's go into town and get Shorty some new boots before he goes to see Cam—and an Exacto knife for me. I have a little test I want to run."

17

Bud sat at the kitchen table in the Teewinot Cafe, the Opabinia fossil in one hand and an Exacto knife in the other. A paper towel held tiny scraps of some kind of dark material that he'd scraped off the fossil.

Shorty had stopped at Wydaho Outdoors and bought some new boots like Howie and Bud's, then gone over to the park to meet Cam. Bud and Howie and Doc had spent part of the day getting ready for the next day's hike up Darby Canyon, though there wasn't really all that much to prepare for, mostly just buying food.

They had walked around Driggs some, had lunch at the diner again, and then gone back to the house just in time for the gals to return from their trip to Jackson.

"I didn't know you'd taken up carving," Millie said, coming into the kitchen. "What are you making?"

"It's an Opabinia," Bud replied, holding the fossil up. "How was your trip to the museum?"

"Oh, it was spectacular," Millie replied. "They have some fantastic art, including some life-sized bison. I'm making tea. Would you like some?"

"Sounds good," Bud said as she put two cups of water into the microwave.

She then asked, "What's an Opabinia?"

"It's an ancient sea critter," Bud said. "Shorty knows all about it."

"That Shorty," Millie said, taking teabags from a small box. "He sure doesn't hang out much. I was hoping to ask him about the geology of the Tetons."

"He was hired by the Park Service, so he's actually working," Bud replied, putting the fossil and knife down. "And getting paid, unlike the rest of us."

She replied, "Well, we're getting paid, too, but not in dollars— we're getting paid in scenery. You did bring your camera, didn't you?"

Bud nodded, adding, "I don't mean to imply I should be getting paid, as just being able to come up here is good enough for me. But when Shorty's getting paid for a job, he goes above and beyond, so don't expect to see him around much."

The water now ready, Millie put a teabag in each cup, then asked, "Cream and sugar?"

"Just a little cream," Bud replied. "Actually, I never drink tea, so maybe put in both."

"That way if you don't like the tea, you'll at least have something in it you *do* like, right?" Millie smiled. Opening the sugar bowl, she let out a squeal, then slammed the lid back on, just as Doc walked in.

"There's a horrible bug in there!" She exclaimed.

"Let me see, Mil," Doc said, picking the bowl up and taking off the lid. He stuck his hand inside while Millie jumped back.

"No! Don't let it out!" She warned. "It could bite you!"

"Oh, Mill, it's nothing, just a big millipede," he said, holding it up and laughing. "It's named after you, Millie...millipede..."

"Hand it to me and I'll take care of it," Bud said, as Doc gave him the Hallucigenia. He then began scraping it with the Exacto knife. As small bits came off, he laughed, "It's not real, Mill. It's a fake fossil Shorty left in there."

"I guess I owe Shorty one," she replied with disgust. "Why would anyone put something like that in the sugar bowl? He's lucky I didn't have a heart attack. Just what is it, anyway?"

Doc, putting his arm around her shoulder, said, "It's from long ago, as in half a billion years. Something Shorty's working on. That's all I know."

Bud sipped the tea, trying not to make a face. "What kind of tea is this?"

"It's Typhoo Green Tea," Millie replied. "Good for you, Bud, so drink up—it has antioxidants, improves brain function, and increases fat burning."

"I knew it had to be good for me," Bud said, slowly sipping the hot brew. "And I like the fat burning part."

"You knew it was good for you because of how bad it tastes, right?" Doc added. "I personally won't touch the stuff. Sounds like Mill conned you into thinking you were getting a real cup of tea, eh?"

"I did no such thing," Millie replied. "I never said he was getting anything real. But that thing in the sugar bowl, we have several almost just like it, except ours *are* real."

"You have fossils?" Bud asked. "Where did you get fossils?"

"We stopped at this place in Jackson, one of those topsy-turvy houses. They're shutting it down and were selling everything at half-off. It's being torn down for a subdivision or something," Millie replied, then yelled into the living room. "Maureen, do you have those fossils handy?"

"What's a topsy-turvy house? Is that a yoyo trick?" Howie asked, having just entered the kitchen.

Millie replied, "You know, one of those so-called 'mystery houses.' They were really popular in the late 1940s and 50s, when people were just beginning to do road trips, or 'See the USA in your Chevrolet' kind of things. After WWII, people were more prosperous and started traveling, or happy motoring, as they called it, and these mystery houses began to spring up everywhere—or at least that's what the guy running it told us."

"What was the mystery?" Doc asked.

"From the outside, it looks like a normal house, but when you go inside, everything's off-kilter, all tilted. I mean, *it's* all normal, but *you're* off kilter and tilted, like you're walking at an angle."

Maureen came into the kitchen with Wilma Jean, who was

carrying a small bright red plastic bag with the words, "Teton Mystery House."

Millie added, "It was very believable, but I know it has to be based on some kind of optical illusion. This old guy took us on the tour, even though he said it was closed. He dropped a tennis ball, and we watched it roll uphill. He said it had been unknowingly built in a vortex and the owners had eventually abandoned it because of all the weirdness."

"And the weirdest thing of all," Doc said, "Was how all these mystery houses just happen to occur suspiciously near interstate interchanges or in tourist hangouts."

"And they're building a subdivision there? I wouldn't want to buy one of those houses," Howie said. "I wonder how big the vortex is."

"Oh, for crying out loud," Maureen said. "You sound like you believe in such things."

"There are many mysteries in the universe," Howie replied. "But let's see these fossils. Were they expensive?"

"No," Maureen said. "He gave them to us. He said he needed to get rid of them as he was clearing everything out. We brought them to show Shorty."

Wilma Jean handed Howie a small fossil, who, after examining it, said, "Wow, this is really cool. What a strange-looking little creature."

He handed it to Bud, who immediately began scraping its back with the Exacto knife. As small pieces of a dark material spalled off, he said, "Howie, I think this is the same deal as the fossils we have."

"So, you're thinking they're not real?" Howie asked.

"I think they're made of resin, just like on that box label."

"But how would you make such real-looking fossils? You'd need a mold first."

"I don't know anything about manufacturing, but I think you could have some company make a mold and produce these for you. And now some old guy's just giving them away to get rid of them? They have to be from the same source as the ones we have and probably also the one from the Cheyenne rock show."

"Of all the things one could make, why not make something valuable?" Wilma Jean asked.

"These fossils would be extremely valuable if they were the real deal," Doc replied. "I was reading a bit about them last night on the Internet after everyone went to bed, and the Burgess Shale fossils are actually priceless. They're not for sale, property of the Canadian government."

"Why would they be so valuable?" Millie asked.

Doc replied, "From what I read, they preserve an invaluable glimpse of early life on Earth. They were first discovered in 1909 by a guy with the Smithsonian. He named them after nearby Mount Burgess in the Canadian Rockies. The original critters were buried in an underwater avalanche of fine mud, which preserved the fine details of their soft parts. Before this, only Cambrian fossils with their hard parts had been found. It's kind of like finding an entire fish completely preserved as opposed to finding just its skeleton."

The dogs, who had been following Wilma Jean around, now began barking. Shorty came in the front door and made his way into the kitchen, sitting down and eyeing Bud's tea.

Bud said, "Millie made it. I'm sure she'd be glad to make you a cup."

As Millie jumped up to put a cup of water in the microwave, Shorty said, "Thanks, Millie. I'm tired. It's been a long day. Cam and I again spent the day searching around the flanks of Teewinot for any kind of evidence that would help solve the ranger's death, but we didn't find anything except recent rockfall. This whole thing is getting really tiresome. I'm supposed to be doing geology, not detective work."

As Millie handed him a cup of tea, Shorty added, "I'm going to recommend that we wait another couple of days before going up to Fossil Mountain. Cam wants to go with us, and he can't go right away."

"That's fine by me," Bud replied, handing Shorty the new fossil. "What do you think of this?"

Shorty said, "More Burgess Shale stuff, which means that there had to be a continuum in environments from here to the Canadian Rockies during the Cambrian, which has never been proved before. Where did these come from?"

Millie repeated the story of the mystery house.

Shorty replied, "I drove right by that mystery house the other day. It's south of Jackson, on the way to Hoback Junction." Making a face as he sipped the tea, he asked, "Where in hellsbells did they get fossils like this? And they just gave them to you? These could be a major breakthrough in geology. We need to find where they originally came from."

"I think they came from some manufacturing facility," Bud replied, pointing to the shreds of material on the napkin. "I don't think they're real, Shorty."

Shorty held a fossil up to examine it more closely, then said, "Bud, I don't think it's possible to make a mold that could capture the fine detail in these. Look at the intricacy of the patterns. I just don't think they could be manufactured, though I agree there's something off about them."

Bud replied, "I don't know enough about it to say one way or the other, but I really don't think they're the real deal. I think they're hardened resin. But I'm thinking that maybe it's time to head over the pass and see if we can find this so-called mystery house and find out where the old guy got these fake fossils. Since we're not going up to Fossil Mountain tomorrow, let's go to Jackson."

"Fine by me, as long as we don't get caught in that vortex," Howie said. "I was already in one up in that glider, and I don't think I'm up for another. I think I'm developing aerophobia."

"What's that, sweetie?" Maureen asked sympathetically.

"Fear of drafts," Howie replied.

"Drafts? Not fear of flying?" Bud asked. "I'm kind of averse to flying, though it's not really a phobia yet."

"Aerophobia is a fear of drafts," Howie replied. "Fear of flying is aviophobia, which also applies to even thinking about flying, which can be as scary as being on the flight itself if you have aviophobia."

"And what's the fear of buffalos called?" Shorty asked. "Buffalo-phobia? Bisonphobia?"

"I don't know," Howie replied. "But as for your buffalo thing being the longest sentence on Earth, well, there's hippopotomonstros-esquippedaliophobia, which is one of the longest words in the dictionary."

"What the heck does that mean?" Doc asked, laughing.

"Fear of long words," Howie said. "Ironic, eh?"

"I've developed a new phobia in just the past day, Howie, but I don't know what it's called," Bud said. "Some kind of yoyophobia."

"What's it like?" Howie asked.

"I'm getting to where I'm afraid to throw the yoyo because I worry it will have some kind of knot and come back and hit me in the face. Just today, I've had eight close encounters so far. I'm getting afraid to throw it."

"Close encounters of the yoyo kind?" Doc laughed.

"Look, Bud," Howie replied. "The only way to get rid of your yoyophobia is to stop worrying about it. If you believe it will happen, it will. Worst comes to worst, you get a bonk on the head, but just remember, once you get a scar you've become a real yoyo player. Or you could always wear a helmet with a face guard. Just don't get a metal yoyo."

"Thanks for the advice, Howie," Bud replied. "I'll get a custom face mask and some bulletproof glasses next time we're in town, or maybe just some custom-made bulletproof mouth guards."

"No problem. Let me know if I can be of further help. But I don't know about doing this mystery house thing, as I'm pretty sure I now have vortexphobia."

"Well, Howie," Shorty replied. "You don't have to go inside. You can hang out outside and make sure nothing happens. But speaking of such, there appears to be another kind of vortex surrounding that plaque Winnie threw into the river, and it might have something to do with the ranger's death."

Dumping what was left of his tea into the sink, Shorty added, "Let's go out to eat, and I'll tell you about it over dinner."

18

Bud was again leading a parade over Teton Pass. He and Howie and Doc were in his old FJ while Shorty, who was driving the park pickup, had left them in the dust coming up the pass.

The plan was to meet at the Teton Mystery House south of Jackson, though Bud wasn't real sure where it was, even though Millie had described how to get there. He'd had trouble following her description, as Lindie, somehow knowing he was leaving her behind, had been trying to get in his lap.

The gals had once again decided to go do their own thing, saying they wanted to take the dogs hiking up Teton Canyon, then tour the vodka distillery.

Now coming down the Jackson side of the pass, Howie asked, "Bud, do you think Winnie had anything to do with the theft of the plaque she dumped in the river? I mean, if Cam told Shorty it had been stolen in July of 1977, maybe she helped. She would've probably been in her 20s about then, based on her telling us she's now 71. She said she and Marty climbed the Grand Teton a number of times, and she might have climbed it with him or even alone and carried it down."

"It's very possible," Bud replied. "Cam said it had been placed on the top of the Grand in 1929 after the Wyoming Legislature passed a resolution declaring Owen and Spalding the first to summit it in 1898. Apparently it had been kind of controversial, with some guys with the Hayden Survey claiming they'd first climbed it in 1872, and there was also a U.S. Army surgeon named William Kieffer who claimed to have climbed it in 1893. I guess none of the latter guys could substantiate their claims, so the legislature went with the Owen-Spalding bunch."

"But why would she or anyone else steal the plaque?" Doc asked.

"Maybe they disagreed that Owen and Spalding were the first," Bud replied. "But they'd need to have a kind of vested interest to haul something that heavy down."

"And to climb the peak in the first place," Howie added. "It's not a casual walk in the park."

"Cam said there's been a long-standing reward out for the plaque by some guy who was a descendent of Owen," Bud said. "Apparently the plaque had been bolted into a rock, as well as cemented in, so whoever took it was pretty dedicated to the idea."

"Maybe it was just someone who didn't like seeing it up there," Doc said. "They felt it ruined the view or something, wasn't natural."

"The funny thing is," Bud added, slowing as they reached the town of Wilson. "Even if the Owen-Spalding party was the first whites, they weren't the actual first people to climb it. There's a stone enclosure near the top that was there when they went up. Shorty said it was probably used by the local Natives for vision quests."

"So, the plaque is kind of pretentious in the sense that it discounts the Native people," Doc said. "The entire argument of who was first is kind of ironic, if you ask me. Probably a boy named Sioux, like in that old Johnny Cash song, you know, S-i-o-u-x."

Bud groaned, but Howie, ignoring Doc's bad pun, said, "My vote's on the Hayden Survey guys, other than the Natives, of course. The survey went all over the West and climbed lots of mountains." He pointed to the nearby wetlands. "Look you guys, a mama and baby moose!"

Bud slowed as they crossed the bridge over the Snake River, then continued on. He said, "Shorty said Cam was shocked to see the plaque, as he figured it was long gone. He wanted to know where it came from, but Shorty just said we found it by the river, as he didn't want to implicate Winnie without knowing more. But he also said Cam told him the whole affair was still quite contentious around Jackson, even given the long time that's passed. I guess it's a big honor to have been the first to climb the Grand Teton."

"I'd be honored to even climb it once," Doc replied. "Yet alone be the first. The whole world would be amazed."

Now in Jackson, they came to the intersection with the main north-south highway, where Bud turned south and continued on out of town.

"Millie said this rural area is called South Park. We'll cross the Snake twice more, and the Mystery House will be after the second bridge on the left, by Horse Creek Road. She said there's an old restaurant near it."

"This is the opposite direction of the museum," Howie noted. "I wonder why they were out this way."

"Millie told me they were scoping out the river because they want to go rafting," Doc said.

"For some reason, I get the feeling they know how to have fun a lot better than we do," Bud remarked.

"Maybe it's because they work harder than we do," Doc said. "Work hard, play hard, right?"

"Hardly work is better in my book," Howie replied. "But actually, work is defined as force times distance. It's a measure of the energy expended in applying a force to move an object."

"So one's not working unless they're moving stuff?" Doc asked. "There's Shorty's truck."

Bud pulled off the highway next to Shorty, who was standing next to a dilapidated sign taking photos. The sign had a giant arrow that pointed to an overgrown parking lot in front of a small decrepit-looking building. It read:

Entrance Teton Mystery House

What is it?
A Wonder of Nature
Amazing
Entertaining for Young and Old
Bring Your Camera

They all got out and walked to the small building, which had been partly built into the foot of the hill and was surrounded by weeds, and which looked about as dilapidated as the sign. Next to its front door, also hand-lettered, was another sign:

What Is It?

Frankly, we don't exactly know, but within a small circular area surrounding the Mystery House you will both see and feel various physical disturbances not found in normal locations.

The fact that these strange phenomena may be photographed from any angle rules out the possibility of optical illusion, however we know of no scientifically acceptable explanation for the phenomena.

We know you will be entertained and feel your visit was time well spent. Be sure to bring your camera. No one will believe the pictures you have but you will have some wonderful arguments while showing them!

It's confusing. It's educational. It's fun. It's a short walk. And there is no danger. Enjoy your visit!

"This is starting to feel kind of spooky and weird," Howie moaned. "I don't think I'm gonna go in there."

"I don't think any of us are going in," Shorty replied, taking more photos. "It's closed."

"Looks like a mystery you won't be able to solve, Sheriff," Howie said. "And I won't say I'm sorry to not step into the vortex."

"I'm not giving up that easily," Bud replied, noting a small wiry man coming their way from the nearby restaurant. "Especially since that fellow looks like he may know something about it. Maybe he can let us in."

As he came closer, Bud could see the man was bald and had a gold tooth that flashed in the sun when he tilted his head just right.

He wore a dark suit jacket that shone with age, along with blue jeans and beat-up cowboy boots.

Seeing Shorty's camera, he said angrily, "This is private property. No photos allowed! Give me that!"

He grabbed the camera and quickly stuck it in his jacket pocket.

Shorty, dumbfounded, finally managed to say, "But it says to bring your camera, though that one actually belongs to the Park Service."

No one said a word for a moment, and Bud was beginning to suspect a confrontation was brewing when Howie finally said, "I had no idea that demanding that people give you their stuff was acceptable behavior. This is going to save me a fortune on groceries!"

Bud could see the man's demeanor visibly change, and he began laughing. He returned the camera to Shorty, slapping him on the shoulder like he was an old buddy.

"I apologize. I get kind of crotchety when I think I'm gonna miss my favorite TV show," he said. "I surmise you're here to try to solve the unsolvable mystery. I guess I can let you in, but you can't stay long. I told myself I wasn't giving any more tours, since it's sold."

"We'll just take a quick look, if that's OK," Bud replied. "What's your favorite show?"

"Scooby-Doo—and this episode is a real special one called *The Mystery Manse Mashup*. Five bucks each. I'm Eddie. Follow me."

19

Eddie opened the creaky door, then led them inside. It took awhile for their eyes to get used to the musty darkness, the building's only light coming in through several windows that were skewed to the floor at an odd angle.

"I think I feel a little sick," Howie whispered. "It's like being on a carnival ride."

Referring to a sign on the wall that read, *No Running or Jumping*, Doc said, "I couldn't run or jump if I tried. I can barely stand up."

Everyone looked like they were standing at an angle to the house itself, an illusion that left Bud wanting to grab onto something, or at least lean on a wall for support.

Eddie said, "What you see lies well-beyond the scope of modern science. But don't be scared, even though gravity is leaking out of the room, there's no danger. Nobody understands how these vortexes work or where they come from."

Seeing Shorty taking photos, he added, "Take as many photos as you wish," to which Shorty replied, "Vortices, not vortexes."

Eddie now took a ball from his pocket and rolled it on the floor.

"It's rolling uphill!" Howie exclaimed, acting like he was almost ready to hyperventilate.

"And watch this," Eddie added, pouring water from a jug sitting on the floor. "It, too, will run uphill, defying gravity."

"How?" Howie asked.

Eddie, looking amused, replied, "It's a mystery. No one in the history of humankind has figured it out, not even the most brilliant scientists, of which there have been many come to unravel the mysteries here. There's even a rumor that Einstein himself visited once and left in frustration."

Doc replied, "If true, he was probably frustrated that anyone would believe in such things."

Eddie, giving him a look, asked, "How would *you* explain this, Mr. Logical?" He then began walking up one of the walls, saying, "One might try to explain how the effect is produced, but knowing the truth will not lesson the enjoyment of the experience, in fact, it becomes more fun the more you know. No good optical illusion is ever ruined by the truth."

"So, it *is* an optical illusion, then," Shorty said, grinning. "But of course it is. A form of spatial distortion. We cling to a false notion of normal space, even though the environment says otherwise. Everybody looks like they're standing at an impossible angle, and you can lean into space without falling."

"The alien vortex is very powerful," Doc added, grinning. "A great beam of high-velocity soft electrons exits the earth through it. And it becomes a social experience as we all share the same illusions. The Mystery House is a sociological experiment that we in Western Civilization should not let go unheeded lest we lose our bearings. It tests our commitment to reality as we challenge our spatial references. But beware of those spots where more than one vortex is tangled up with others, as they can be very dangerous."

Eddie, looking dubiously at Doc, said, "Are you having fun or not?"

"Sure," Doc replied. "But are you willing to tell us how it's done?"

Eddie sighed. "I don't want to miss my show, but I still have a few minutes. Since this place is no longer a going concern, I'll tell you all about it. The only vortex here is in your mind. Buckle up and I'll tell you how it came to be."

"Tell us how it's done, first," Doc replied. "Then you can give us its history. That way, if you run out of time before Scooby-Doo, we won't be left in the dark."

"Fair enough," Eddie said, sitting in a chair that was leaning into a wall as if it would fall over any minute.

"You'll first notice that the house itself is built into a hill, and we cleverly disguised its construction by planting bushes and such around it. See, one side of the house itself was built at a tilt of about 25 degrees, but you won't notice it because the room is placed along a slope and the landscaping makes it look level. We built the slant of the ceiling to look normal, and even the windows are distorted. You have to make it look like it's not tilted. Then when you walk in, you're actually still level, but the room isn't. Because you weren't aware it would be tilted, your mind tries to make it all work, and you lose your frame of reference. You think *you're* tilted, but it's actually the house itself."

"Very clever," Bud said. "But now tell us how it came to be."

Eddie continued. "When I was a kid, my folks always took me and my sister on a summer vacation. This particular year, I was eight years old, and we decided to go to Yellowstone. We lived in Ohio, so it was a bit of a drive, and we always camped out on the way to wherever we were going.

"My dad was pretty creative—let's just call it that—and if he couldn't find a public place to camp, like a fairgrounds in some town or other, he'd always go for private land that looked abandoned, especially places that were for sale, as he figured nobody would be around much.

"Well, we were almost to Yellowstone, when my mom wanted to stop, and my dad saw this for sale sign at this place by the road that looked pretty nice, lots of trees, so we stopped and got out.

"My dad and mom walked around, then all of a sudden they started acting real weird, like they were drunk or something. They were carrying on all tipsy-turvy like they could barely stand up, holding onto each other, then they yelled for me to come over and help them, 'cause they were stuck. I grabbed my dad's arm, and he was hanging onto my mom, and I pulled them back over to the car. I was scared to death.

"Well, my dad said they'd been caught in a vortex. I kind of had an idea what a vortex was, as we'd just stopped back in Nebraska at a mystery house, and I didn't like it one bit, I just wanted to get out of there.

"But my folks said they were going to buy the place, so, the next few days we camped there and forgot all about Yellowstone, making a deal with the owner, and before a week was up, we owned it. I think they may have paid less than a thousand dollars for it—this was back in the early 70s.

"My dad took my sis and my mom back to Cheyenne, where they caught the train and went home while he and I stayed and built this mystery house that you're in right now. My dad was an electrician and wired people's houses, so that's how he was able to just up and quit and stay out here, 'cause he owned his own business.

"He later went home to help move, but only after it took us all summer to build this thing, just him and me, and if it had been a regular house it would've fallen down, 'cause neither of us knew anything about construction. He later admitted there was no vortex —he and my mom were just hamming it up. They'd decided to buy it the minute they saw it.

"So, I grew up here, and I've lived here all my life in a little trailer back in the woods a ways, which my dad brought in while we got the mystery house going. He promised my mom a real house, but he never came through. But at least neither of them had to work, as the mystery house ended up paying the bills. And now that it's sold, I'm a rich old sunuvagun, even after I split the money with my sis. I'm going to go on over to Idaho Falls in a few days, where my kids both live."

Eddie now led them outside, locking the door. "I gotta go, fellas. Thanks for stopping by."

"One last question, if you don't mind," Bud said. "Our wives stopped by here yesterday, and they showed us some fossils you gave them. That was really nice of you, but Shorty here is a geologist, and he's wondering where they came from. Would you mind sharing that?"

Eddie didn't hesitate. "I got those from the guy who just bought the property. He's a developer, and he's going to tear the Mystery House down and build houses here. He told me he had a friend he got them from, and if I wanted to sell what he had left I could. I took them, but I'm not really into retail, too much trouble, so I gave them away. Your wives are a nice bunch."

"What was his name?" Bud asked.

"Parker Watson. He's well-known around here. He built the Teton Flats, which is a big apartment complex on the edge of town."

"Teton Flats?" Shorty asked.

"Yeah, Parker thinks *flats* means *apartments*, which is a joke on him as the rest of us see how it doesn't fit with the Tetons. But he doesn't care what anyone thinks. All he cares about is money. He overpaid for this place or I would never have sold it to him. As my Swedish grandma used to say, 'Är huvudet dumt får kroppen lida—If the head is dumb the body will suffer.' He doesn't appear to be suffering yet, though, not that I can tell, but his time will come."

"My dad must've been part-Swedish," Shorty said. "'Cause he always told me that if you're gonna be dumb, you gotta be tough."

"Same idea," Eddie replied. "But I gotta run."

"Thanks for everything, Eddie. *But it looks like we've got another mystery on our hands. And we would've gotten away with it, if it weren't for those meddling kids,*" Bud said, grinning.

"*Ta-ta-ta-ta-ta-taa! Puppy Power!*" Eddie said with surprise, winking at Bud. "Another Scooby-Doo fan! *Ruh-roh.*"

He then headed back to the restaurant, patting his pocket full of five-dollar bills.

20

It was evening, and everyone was still in town running various errands, leaving Bud and Wilma Jean and the dogs alone at the Teewinot Cafe.

Wilma Jean had offered earlier to make dinner for the gang, and after playing ball with the dogs in the back yard, Bud had gone into the kitchen to see if she needed help.

She stood over a big stainless steel pot on the stove, its contents bubbling, the rising steam making her curly dark hair even curlier than usual.

"Whatcha cookin'?" Bud asked, putting his arm around her waist while doing a Walk the Dog with the yoyo in his other hand.

"Hon, I know you're not crazy about seafood, but everyone else wanted clam chowder. It's a recipe I got from Maureen, and it should be really tasty. I'm going to put a pan of enchiladas in the oven for you after I get this going."

Bud squeezed her shoulder, saying, "Thanks, I appreciate that. I never acquired a taste for seafood, since the only kind we could get when I was a kid was the frozen stuff. My mom used to feed us breaded shrimp, and I would eat the breading and feed the dogs the shrimp under the table."

"So, you learned to feed the dogs under the table as a kid?" She asked. "I'm not surprised. But this does kind of smell good, doesn't it?"

Bud leaned over the pot, watching as she slowly stirred what looked like clams in and out of a thick white paste. He actually didn't smell anything, the whole shebang reminding him of when they'd made plaster of Paris in grade school, except they hadn't heated it up.

"Aren't you supposed to shell the clams first?" Bud asked. "I mean, I'm not a clam chowder expert by any means, but aren't the shells kind of hard to eat?"

"Hon," she replied with a hint of exasperation. "The shells open when the clams are done, then you discard them. Hand me that box of corn starch over there, please. I need to thicken this up a little. And I know I said clam chowder, but Maureen's recipe is more like a bouillabaisse."

"What's that?" Bud asked, watching as she poured in more corn starch, making the sauce even thicker.

"It's a French soup. Fish and vegetables, but Maureen's recipe uses clams and whatever other seafood you have on hand."

"People typically have seafood on hand?" Bud asked. "But what are those little double shelled things bubbling with the clams? The ones with the grooves in the shell?"

"Brachiopods."

"Brachiopods? Aren't they extinct? I thought the only known brachiopods were fossils."

"No, Bud, they still exist," Wilma Jean replied with a hint of frustration. "The Japanese eat them. They come from cold waters, like near the Arctic."

As Bud watched, the bouillabaisse became thicker and thicker, until Wilma Jean could barely stir it. She then took the pot from the stove and poured the contents into a baking pan, spooning the clams and brachiopods into layers, then placing it all into the oven.

"Did I say bouillabaisse?" Wilma Jean asked. "I meant casserole."

"Yum," Bud said. "Clam-brachiopod bake. But there's no way you can get the shells out now. I guess you pick around them when eating, eh? But let's get to the enchiladas. What ingredients do you need?"

She sighed, "I'm tired. That was way too much work. Sorry, hon. I'm going to go lay down for awhile."

As Wilma Jean left the kitchen, Hoppie and Pierre following her, Bud suddenly felt abandoned. He didn't think he could gag seafood down even if it were cooked by the world's best chef, and this casserole stuff didn't look too tasty, even if his wife had made it.

He went and sat on the couch in the now-dark living room, Lindie jumping up by his side. Maybe he could run into town and grab something to eat there, he thought, leaning back and closing his eyes, his stomach starting to growl. He wondered when the gang was coming back.

Just then, Shorty came in, carrying a box with *Wydaho Outdoors* stamped on it.

"I bought some nice boots at that place you recommended, Bud, but man, talk about expensive! Now we can all go hiking and look for fossils."

"That's great, Shorty," Bud replied.

"Why are you sitting in the dark, and what smells so good?" Shorty asked, walking into the kitchen. "Smells just like fossiliferous stew, like baked brachiopods."

He came back into the living room, turned on a light, and sat in a chair across from Bud, then began singing:

> It's a long way from Amphioxus. It's a long way to us.
> It's a long way from Amphioxus to the meanest human
>   cuss.
> Well, it's goodbye to fins and gill slits, and it's welcome
>   lungs and hair!
> It's a long, long way from Amphioxus, but we all came
>   from there.

Laughing, he added, "I've had that stupid song stuck in my head all day. It's the first song one learns when starting a paleontology career. It's sung to *It's a Long Way to Tipperary*, that old song from WWI. It's been around since the 1920s and has lots more verses. But say, Bud, did you know that jellyfish have survived for over 500 million years, in spite of having no brain, heart, or eyes? Pretty impressive, eh? That fact should give hope to many people."

Bud laughed, though he felt something was off. He wondered if Shorty hadn't maybe taken the tour of the vodka distillery or something.

"Shorty, I don't understand the song. What's an Amphioxus?" Bud asked.

"The amphioxus *Branchiostoma* is the earliest known chordate, Bud, or critter with a spinal column, though it was a primitive one. The cephalochordates, or amphioxus species, were our earliest vertebrate ancestors. But it smells like that fossiliferous stew is done."

Bud followed Shorty back into the kitchen, where he got an oven mitt and took the baking pan from the oven.

"Let me find my rock hammer and we can dig in," Shorty said and was soon chipping at the cooling slab, which was now hard as a rock.

"Maybe we'll find an Hallucigenia, Bud, or an Opabinia, if we're lucky."

"Nothing in there but clams and brachiopods," Bud replied.

"It looks like it's been metamorphosed, Buddy," Shorty said, holding up a chunk of what looked like white rock. "Exposed to very high temperatures. We're not likely to find any fossils."

"Shorty, we have lots of fossils already."

"I know you think they're fake, Bud, but they can't be," Shorty said, hammering again on the slab. "The features are too fine to manufacture. You could never make a mold that finely detailed."

"But you saw how I was able to scratch stuff off them, and it wasn't sandstone or anything like that," Bud said. "But I think there's more going on here than someone digging fossils in the park and illegally selling them."

"Who would be dumb enough to buy fake fossils?"" Shorty asked.

"About any non-geologist," Bud replied. "And Shorty, if they are fake, you've been half-fooled, too, and you're an expert."

"No, the jury's still out, Bud. Remember I said they seemed off and I wanted to send them to a lab? I have my doubts, but they do look real."

Wilma Jean was now in the kitchen in her PJs, admonishing them for making so much noise. She began poking Bud in the ribs.

"You need to go sleep on the couch," she said. "I really need to get some rest, and you've been tossing and turning and talking in your sleep."

Bud, now beginning to wake, realized he was in bed, Shorty nowhere near, Lindie sitting nearby looking at him with concern.

It had all been a dream, he realized, taking a blanket and pillow and heading for the couch. They'd come home from the mystery house, and Howie had made another nice dinner, after which they'd all talked for awhile on the back deck, then everyone had gone to bed.

There had been no casserole or fossils or Shorty singing crazy songs, Bud mused, now trying to get comfortable on the couch, Lindie at his feet.

But just as he was beginning to drift off back to sleep, he noticed a shadowy figure standing outside by the sidelight window, a figure that was now quietly tapping on the door, as if asking to be let in.

He thought for a minute he was still dreaming, as Lindie didn't seem at all alarmed. Finally, he slipped out from under the blanket and went to the door and unlocked it, looking outside.

It was Doc!

"Thanks for letting me in," Doc whispered. "That dang moose is back, and I thought for sure I was gonna die out there."

"How did you get locked out?" Bud asked.

"I went out to look at the stars, well, and to have a little bit of a cigar, as I couldn't sleep. The door locks itself when you go out if you forget to turn the latch. But what are you doing sleeping on the couch?"

"I was having a weird dream, keeping Wilma Jean awake, and she gave me the boot," Bud explained. "But Doc, since you can't sleep either, let's put our heads together—they say two heads are better than one."

"I'd hate to see what your donor card looks like, Bud," Doc joked. "What do you have in mind?"

"Let me grab my laptop, then we'll go into the kitchen where we won't bother anyone. You can help me do a little research over a hot drink."

"Sounds good," Doc replied. "As long as you don't try to make me drink any of that green tea." He studied Bud for a moment, then added, "And I'll try to ignore the fact that you're wearing those silly Scooby-Doo PJs."

21

Bud sat at the kitchen table, his laptop in front of him, sipping a cup of peppermint tea with cream in it. Doc was drinking something he'd just made in a large mug embossed with the words, *Grand Teton National Park.*

"That smells good," Bud said. "What is it?"

"It helps me sleep. It's called a Shumway Espresso Martini. My good friends out in Georgia, Mike and Joan Venator, sent me the recipe."

"What's in it?" Bud asked. "If it's espresso, it's not going to help you sleep."

"Actually, it has the opposite effect of what you'd think," Doc replied. "It's made with one measure of Grey Goose Vodka, one measure of Bailey's Irish Cream, one measure of Kahlua, and two measures of espresso with cream, like in a latte."

Bud asked, "Why do you call it a Shumway Espresso Martini? I mean, I get the espresso and martini part, but why the Shumway?"

"The last thing you add is a dollop of vanilla-bean ice cream."

Bud laughed. "Well, I like that last part, but the other ingredients would for sure put me to sleep, except the espresso. But listen here,

Doc. I keyed in the words from the box in the glider, and this is what it came up with."

Prima Creator Value is a standard resin that works well with DLP 3D printers that operate in the range of 395-405 nm. It comes in a range of different colors and the parts it produces are quite impressive. Of the standard resins on the market, this particular resin performs very well in terms of capturing fine details. Sharp edges, tiny patterns, and all other details found on models meant for resin 3D printing are reproduced really well.

"Hot dog!" Doc replied. "3D printing! The fossils were made with a printer! Who wudda thunk it?"

"OK, now look at this," Bud pointed to his laptop screen, then to the two fossils he'd just taken from the sugar bowl.

"I entered the word *Opabinia*, and this is the exact duplicate of the fossil we have here, I mean exact. Same orientation, everything. And the same with the Hallucigenia. Someone used these photos from the Burgess Shale to create a template for their 3D printer."

"I wonder how difficult making a template would be," Doc replied.

"Not very hard if you contact the Smithsonian," Bud replied. "Look here. I entered the words *Hallucigenia template*, and came up with this. Too easy."

Welcome to the 3D Scanning Frontier
   The 3D Program is a small group of technologists working within the Smithsonian Institution Digitization Program Office. We focus on developing solutions to further the Smithsonian's mission of "the increase and diffusion of knowledge" through the use of three-dimensional capture technology, analysis tools, and our distribution platform.

"Doc, they have entire collections of templates you can download for 3D printers—corals, dinosaurs, various fossils, models of the Space Shuttle, and even Neil Armstrong's spacesuit! It says it's open access and public domain—anyone can use these. They even have a

Tyrannosaurus rex skull and a ladybug, and lots of art objects, thousands of images."

"So, someone downloaded the Smithsonian's Burgess Shale templates, made them with a 3D printer, then started selling them. But who would be dumb enough to buy a fake fossil?"

Bud replied, "Apparently, enough people to make it worth their time. Even Shorty wasn't convinced they weren't real, though he had his doubts. It's the fine detail."

"If the fossils are fake, that means there's no fossil site in the Tetons after all, and Shorty and Cam are on a wild-goose chase," Doc said. "Does this mean we don't need to hike up to Fossil Mountain? I'm kind of wondering if I would be able to do that anyway, as I'm not in the greatest shape. You know, I'm pretty active, but it mostly amounts to puttering around in my hobby orchard."

"Well," Bud replied. "The fossils may not be illegal in terms of coming from the park, but it's certainly not ethical to sell fakes, especially if you're telling people they're from the Tetons. But fake fossils versus real fossils would shift the focus of everything. Do you think the guy at the Mystery House's story about the developer giving him the fossils is true?"

"He seems honest enough," Doc replied. "Anyone with the mindset of a Scooby-Doo fan is probably OK."

"The mindset?" Bud asked, looking questioningly at Doc.

"You know, the ability to get involved with things at that level. Geez, Bud, put me on the spot here."

Bud laughed. "I know, I know. But I like the show. It makes solving mysteries seem like fun, which it rarely is."

"Agreed," Doc replied. "At least in my brief experience trying to solve mysteries with you. But trying to figure things out *is* interesting, at least, or I wouldn't be staying up all night like this."

"The main problem here, Doc, is the ranger's death. If it were just a bunch of fake 3D printer fossils, things wouldn't be so serious. But somehow it seems all rolled up together. And I can't figure out why there would be strange booming sounds—they were heard before the ranger disappeared and also by the people who Shorty helped rescue."

"What was the ranger's name again?" Doc asked.

"Marty Langford."

"And didn't you say that ranger fellow named Jamie accused you and Howie of having something to do with his grave over on the flanks of Teewinot? What was that all about?"

"We found what looked to be a grave, and the ranger accused us of a bunch of different things. He interrogated us and wanted to arrest us. But you know, Doc, when I asked him if it was Marty's grave, he sort of went white on us, which was odd. I mean, he seemed like he was accusing us of being involved in Marty's death, yet when we mentioned it, he acted like he hadn't considered the grave might be Marty's. It was odd."

"Sounds like it," Doc replied. "But maybe you're making assumptions there that don't hold, Bud. You've been in this game long enough to know things aren't always what they seem. Maybe there's something else going on there, something not even related to Langford's death."

"I don't know," Bud replied. "He accused us of discharging a firearm in a national park, transporting stolen material through a national park, disposing of a body in a national park, and theft of government property. It could be something else, except how do you account for the part about disposing of a body? Wouldn't that mean Langford's?"

"It seems like it," Doc said. "But be careful about making assumptions, is all I can say."

"But what else could it be?" Bud persisted. "And the ranger, Jamie, he seemed awfully eager to implicate Howie and I, almost like he wanted to pin it on us, even without evidence. I mean, Utah plates? That could be anyone."

"Maybe he's the guilty one, did you consider that? He's being diversionary."

Bud thought for a moment, then said, "I'm not sure he even knew

Marty was dead at that point, Doc, which would account for his reaction. But say, just a hunch, but Mason has Utah plates."

"Who's Mason?"

"He's the one with the glider that had the 3D resin box in it. And he told Howie he wanted to check out Fossil Mountain, though he didn't exactly call it that, but he did a low pass over some people digging there."

"Could've been a coincidence." Doc replied. "If he saw people, he was probably curious. It doesn't mean he was involved in anything. You know, some people will read the sign, but others have to touch the paint."

"What does that mean?" Bud asked, sipping the last of his tea.

"Some people are overly curious and get involved in things they don't need to. Why did you guys come up here to the Tetons in the first place, anyway?"

"Good question. I really don't know. I think Shorty told Cam I was a good detective, then this Marty guy got killed, and Cam thought I could be of use. But he changed his mind after we got here."

"So Marty was killed before you came up?"

Bud paused, then said, "You know, Doc, I actually don't think he was. He was just missing. Shorty found out he was dead after we got here. And I got the feeling Cam didn't want us involved after Langford's death."

"Maybe he was worried about liability, or like Howie's always asking, worried there might be gunplay."

"Sounds logical," Bud replied. "And then there's the fact that Langford, according to his ex-wife Winnie, was involved in fighting an expansion of the Ghee. Howie and I walked in on an argument between the Wydaho Outdoors owner and the developer involved in that expansion, and it was pretty contentious. Ironically enough, that developer, a man named Parker, was the same one who bought the Mystery House. But are you getting tired yet?"

"A little, but not bad. And you?"

Howie now poked his head around the corner. "Did I hear my name? What are you guys doing up so late?"

"Just talking, Howie," Bud replied. "Did we wake you?"

"No, I couldn't sleep," Howie said.

"Seems to be the problem du jour," Doc said.

"You would mean du nuit," Howie replied. "That's French for *night*. But you guys are in for a big treat."

"How so?" Bud asked.

Howie continued. "Well, remember when you were a kid, and you went out running around at night and your parents didn't know about it? It was a big adventure. Well, just now, I was in bed, trying to sleep, and all I could think about was the big night sky and all the stars hanging over the house, just right up there. I want to get my telescope out. It's midnight—the perfect time for star gazing."

Now Maureen was also in the kitchen, wearing her robe and slippers. She asked, "What's going on here?"

"We're going to get my telescope and go out," Howie said excitedly. "Get dressed and come with us. I guess I need to get dressed, too. And Bud..."

"I know, I know, my PJs," Bud replied. "But I want to do one last thing here before we go."

He keyed in the name *Marty Langford*.

Several entries came up, but all were for Marty Langfords in different parts of the country, nothing for Idaho or Wyoming. He finally saw a site that appeared to be the genealogy of the Langford family and clicked on it. A screen with their family tree came up with Marty Langford's name highlighted.

After studying it for awhile, Bud clicked on another site. Finally, he said, "Fellas, check this out. Marty was the descendent of a guy named Nathaniel Langford, who was born in the 1800s. I click on his name, and I get an extensive article about him—he was a famous Hayden Survey explorer. Weren't two Hayden Survey fellows among those who supposedly first climbed the Grand? Do you suppose that's Marty's great-great whatever?"

"Bingo!" Doc said. "A connection that might explain the missing plaque."

Bud hesitated. "I'm not really sure it's the right guy. I need to do more research."

"No more research needed tonight, it's too late, Sheriff," Howie said. "Let's go look at the stars."

"That moose is still out there," Doc said.

Howie replied, "We can go up Teton Canyon—no light pollution, and it's not far."

"Sounds like a plan," Shorty said, now also in the kitchen. "We can have a star party." Eyeing Bud's PJs, he added, "Or if nobody wants to get dressed, a pajama party."

22

After all was said and done, Bud and Howie ended up being the only ones up for a midnight star party, everyone else opting instead for a good night's sleep, especially Doc after finishing his Shumway Espresso Martini.

Bud was wide-awake after drinking the tea, and he and Howie drove in the FJ up the road to Teton Canyon, Lindie riding along in the back seat.

"Bud, let's go on up to the Ghee instead," Howie said, referring to what the locals called Grand Targhee Ski Area on Fred's Hill above Teton Canyon. "Did you know that ghee is also a French style of clarified butter?"

"I don't even know what clarified butter is," Bud replied. "But hows come you know so much French these days?"

"I actually don't know what it is either. I just saw it in a cookbook Maureen got from the library."

"Well, let's hope ghee's not to butter what Old Man Green's watermelon spritzer is to drinks," Bud replied. "But I would think that we're less likely to see bears and wolves up there."

"You think so?" Howie asked with concern. "I never even thought of that. Maybe this star party isn't such a good idea after all."

"Don't worry, Howie. It won't be much of a party, anyway, with just you and me."

"And Lindie," Howie added. "She can alert us if there's anything around. We'll be closer to the stars up there, but the moon's going to rise in about an hour, so we need to get going."

They soon climbed the hill to the ski area, where a number of cars were parked in front of the condos, indicating the area had overnight guests, even though it was summer.

"People come up here to ride the lift and hike and mountain bike," Howie said. "I think if we park over by the Stick of Truth, we can slip down the hill a little to where we can't see any lights."

"What's the Stick of Truth?" Bud asked.

"It's a snow-depth indicator. See that big measuring stick thing over there? It has a webcam focused on it and people can look to see how deep the snow is in the winter."

Bud parked nearby and they got out, Howie carrying his telescope, which seemed to Bud to have grown since they'd packed it into the FJ back in Green River.

"How'd your telescope get so big, Howie? It looks like a small howitzer."

"I put it together back at the house, Bud. It comes apart for transporting. Do you mind carrying the tripod?"

They started down the hill, Lindie following, then soon found a place to set up everything. Howie mounted the telescope on the tripod, fiddled with it for awhile, then stood back.

"Man, talk about a starry sky," he said.

"I don't think I've ever seen a sky so dense with stars," Bud replied. "I thought they were really something out in the Big Empty, but this is astounding. It looks like layer after layer."

"Wait until your eyes adapt," Howie said. "You'll see even more. It takes about a half-hour. We're probably seeing a good 5,000 or so stars here, Bud."

"How can you estimate something like that? Nobody could count them all—they're too close together."

"True, but astronomers have their ways. In the average night sky, they say you can see about 2,000 stars, but that includes where there's a bit of haze and light pollution. We have neither of those here, so I'm going for twice that. We have absolutely perfect conditions of darkness and sky clarity and are probably looking at thousands of stars, maybe even up to 10,000."

"And if I understand it right," Bud replied. "We're looking at how they all looked many light years ago, right?"

"Right," Howie replied. "Time long gone into the past. But Bud, take a look at this."

Putting his eye to the telescope, Bud could see a disk-shaped smudge of distant light with a bright center.

"Wow, what is it? It's beautiful." Bud asked.

"It's the Andromeda Galaxy, also called Messier 31, or M31. It's the most distant thing humans can see with the naked eye."

Looking up from the telescope, Bud could barely make out a tiny elliptical smudge in the sky.

"It looks like a milky blur without the telescope," he said.

Howie replied, "It's twice the size of the Milky Way and has a massive star cluster in its center and a supermassive black hole hidden somewhere inside it. It's moving towards us at about 68 miles a second and is going to collide with the Milky Way Galaxy in about 4.5 billion years."

"Better hang onto your hat!" Bud replied.

"It has a disk of blue stars that's encircled by a ring filled with red stars," Howie added. "Bud, we're really lucky to know about these things—they enrich our lives. The people of long ago must've wondered about all this, but they didn't have the answers. It's kind of humbling."

"Agreed, Howie," Bud replied. "And sometimes it's good to feel humility."

"Insignificance."

"Right. It takes the pressure off you when you realize you're just some unimportant creature in a huge magnificent universe."

"True," Howie agreed. "But Bud, I have something that's been bothering me."

"Shoot," Bud replied.

"Well, you know, sometimes when I see you and Doc together and realize what a close friendship you have, I feel a little, well, I'm not sure how to describe it, but maybe jealous, which I don't find very becoming of me. I don't know why I feel that way, because we're good friends, at least I think so, anyway."

Bud laughed. "Howie, you shouldn't feel that way at all. I spend very little time with Doc and a lot of time with you, so it's only natural he and I would interact more when he's around. But a person has room for all kinds of friends in their lives, and it doesn't mean one is any better than the other. You're my very best buddy, but different friends add different things to one's life."

"How so?"

"Well, let's use the analogy of a vehicle. To me, Doc is kind of like the gas you put in your car. He keeps things moving along, especially when I get stuck trying to solve a mystery."

"So what would I be?" Howie asked.

"Well, you're kind of like the front window. You help me see things from a different perspective, like up here looking at galaxies and whatnot. Doc shows up when I'm about to run out of gas, but you're always there for me, looking out."

"What about Shorty?"

"Shorty's kind of like the bumper. He keeps me from crashing and burning and getting myself into too much trouble," Bud laughed. "Maureen and Millie are like the heater and AC and everything that makes the trip comfortable and fun. And Wilma Jean, she's the steering wheel—and the gas pedal, and maybe a few other things as well."

"So who's the brakes?" Howie asked.

"Nobody," Bud replied. "There aren't any."

Howie laughed, but it was short-lived, for he quickly said, "Bud, what's up with Lindie?"

The little dingo was making a low guttural sound that was barely audible, but which soon turned into a full-on growl, her cockles standing up. She came up to Bud for security, standing between his legs.

"There's something nearby, Howie. Maybe we should skedaddle."

"I forgot the bear spray," Howie moaned, picking up the telescope and collapsing the tripod legs.

But before they could head back up the hill to the safety of the FJ, a voice called out so low they could barely make out what it was saying.

"Please help me. I need help."

"There's someone in the trees," Bud said. "Howie, shine your light."

Howie's flashlight revealed a thin, wiry woman leaning against a tree as if she could barely stand, wearing pink polka-dotted pajamas with hiking boots and a small backpack.

"Bud," Howie whispered. "Word must've gotten out about our pajama party!"

"I need to get back to my camp," the woman said quietly, as if not wanting to be overheard by anyone else. "But I'm afraid to go back. Someone's following me, and I think my life may be in danger. I have my cat in my pack, and I need to get him to safety. Can you please help?"

"Howie," Bud said in surprise. "It's Winnie!

23

"Bud?" Winnie asked, incredulous. "It's you guys?"

"Winnie, what's going on?" Bud asked.

Winnie stumbled out from the trees, grabbing onto Bud, who helped steady her.

"Bud, I have Bijou in my pack. Would you mind carrying him? I'm about to collapse."

Bud quickly took the pack, which had the drawstring closed almost all the way, though he could see two eyes glowing in the light, eyes that looked scared.

"Let's get up to the FJ," Bud said, gently swinging the pack over his shoulder as he helped support Winnie. "We're parked just up at the top of the hill here."

They were soon at the FJ, where Bud helped Winnie into the front seat, then handed her the pack as Howie put away the telescope and got into the back with Lindie.

"Now, then, Winnie," Bud said, starting the FJ. "Can you tell us what's going on? Do you want us to take you back to your camp?"

Winnie sighed. "No, not there. I don't know where to go, but not back to camp. They may be waiting for me."

"Who's they?" Howie asked.

"I'm not sure," she replied. "I was in bed, almost asleep, when I heard someone outside talking in a low voice. I couldn't make out much of what they were saying, and I at first thought it was someone camping who needed something. I've had people come ask for stuff at the weirdest hours of the night, things like matches, wood, bandaids, you name it."

Bud could see she had opened the pack enough that Bijou's head could stick out and was petting him.

"Then I heard them say, 'She sleeps in the tent. Hurry and jimmy the door.' I knew someone was trying to break in, so I slipped on my boots, grabbed my pack, which has my keys and ID and bear spray, then stuffed Bijou into it and slipped out the side door and into the bushes, then cut across to the road and started running. I could then hear someone shouting and a vehicle coming, so I ducked into the trees and started going uphill, as I knew I could eventually make it to the ski area and get help."

"Why didn't you go to one of the other campers?" Bud asked. "Wouldn't it be easier than climbing up here through the dark forest?"

"There weren't any other campers," she replied. "We'd just closed the campground that afternoon because of a bear that keeps coming in and raiding tents. I thought at first that's what it was, then I realized there was talking. Anyway, I have a headlamp in my pack, so I got it out so I could see where I was going, but it must've shown where I was, because I could then hear someone following me."

"Someone breaking through the bushes behind you?" Howie asked. "Man, this is scary stuff."

"Yes, I've never been so scared in my life, I can tell you that. I didn't know whether to turn off the light and hide, or just run—I decided to run, which wasn't easy at my age and with this heavy little guy on my back. He must've gotten quite a shaking up. I came up one of the ski runs."

"Do you think it was whoever was breaking into your VW that was following you, or maybe a bear or lion?" Bud asked.

"I don't know, but it easily kept up with me. I'd have to stop to catch my breath, and I could hear it still coming every time."

"Did you see a light?"

"No, which scared me even more, because at that point, I was afraid I'd stirred up something. Like you said, a bear or lion—but lions are stealthy, so I'm thinking a bear. It was too heavy to be a wolf. But I finally got up to where you guys thankfully were. I don't know if I could've made it up to the lodge or not, I'm so tired."

They were now at the bottom of Fred's Hill where the road up Teton Canyon merged with the main road.

"Do you think it's safe to get your VW?" Bud asked. "If so, you could bring it down to where we're staying and park in the drive. You'd be safe there. Or if you prefer, you could come sleep on the couch. Unfortunately, we don't have any spare bedrooms."

"Could Howie ride with me?" Winnie asked. "It would be nice to get my clothes and some food for Bijou. He can sleep in his carrier if I end up on your couch, but my VW has everything I need."

Bud turned down the road to the campground, the FJ bouncing along on the washboards. They soon reached a big sign that read *Campground Closed Due to Bear Activity* hung on a chain lying across the road.

Bud remarked, "Looks like whoever bothered you was in too big of a hurry to put the chain back up."

Howie got out and moved it aside, and they were soon at Winnie's VW bus, where he and Bud got out and carefully walked all around.

Finally, Bud said, "Winnie, it looks like everything's OK, except for the side window, which they managed to break. Howie's cleaning up the glass so you can drive it back to our place. Do you want me to take your tent down?"

"Oh, no, not tonight, Bud," Winnie replied. "I just want to get out of here as quickly as possible. Can Howie ride back with me?"

"Of course," Bud replied. "We can come get the tent tomorrow. They won't need a camp host with the campground closed. And we'll put some cardboard over that window for tonight. Maybe tomorrow we can take it in and get it replaced in Driggs. It's not very secure without it, but you'll be OK camped in our drive."

"I don't know what I would do without you guys," Winnie repeated.

"Winnie, do you have any idea who would be breaking into your bus, and why?"

She was silent for awhile, and Bud had decided she didn't want to talk about it, when she finally replied, "Yes, I think I recognized the voice, though it wouldn't hold up in court. It sounded just like Jamie McKenzie, another ranger Marty worked with sometimes in the park."

"Why would Jamie break into your VW? Was he looking for you, or maybe for something else?"

"Oh, I'm sure he didn't want to find me," she replied. "He and I have had our differences, and he thinks I'm nuts. We got into a yelling match once, and I went after him with my fisticuffs—just to scare him, that's all, I'm actually not violent. This was at Marty's house. Jamie took off, and ever since then, he steers clear of me, which I find kind of ironic, since I'm a 71-year-old grandma and he's a law enforcement officer."

"What were you arguing about, if you don't mind my asking?" Bud asked.

"Nothing very important, Bud. Just an old feud that goes back several generations in his and Marty's families. We can talk about it later, but it actually has nothing to do with anything."

She hesitantly got out of the FJ, putting Bijou into a carrier in the back of her bus. She was soon in the driver's seat, and Howie got in beside her as she started it up.

As they headed out, Howie yelled, "Follow us!"

Bud, now feeling more nervous, being alone and the last one out, started up the FJ, Lindie in the passenger seat. Back where the chain lay by the side of the road, he stopped and got out, hanging it back across the road. As he got back in, he noticed Lindie was staring out the passenger side window, her hackles standing straight up, again making that low guttural growl.

There, not more than 30 feet away, stood a large gray wolf. It paused, eyeing Lindie, then turned on its haunches and headed toward the campground.

Bud watched the graceful animal lope down the road in the rising moonlight, not sure whether to be afraid or to count himself lucky to have seen it.

Maybe both, he sighed, heading on down the road to the Teewinot Cafe.

24

It was still dark when Bud woke. He tried to go back to sleep, but couldn't, so he finally got up and slipped into the kitchen, Lindie at his heels. Not wanting to wake anyone, he made a quick cup of instant coffee in the microwave, poured in some half and half, grabbed a Barkie Biscuit for Lindie, then went out onto the back deck to sit, hoping that the moose wasn't nearby.

He could see the first light of dawn barely outlining the ragged Tetons in the distance, and he thought of Marty Langford, wondering what his life had been like as a ranger in the massive range.

His thoughts then went to Ranger Jamie McKenzie, and he wondered if it had actually been him at the campground or someone else. Now fully awake, he remembered that Winnie was camped in the drive in her VW bus, a fact verified by a hint of light shining from the solar panels on its roof. He then thought he saw light in the bus's interior.

She must be awake, Bud mused, unless she slept with a light on, which he doubted, as electricity was hard to come by in a bus and batteries were expensive.

The song *It's Later than You Think* came to mind, and he began humming the tune, then abruptly quit, not wanting to wake up anyone. Coffee done, he slipped back into the house, made another cup, grabbed his laptop, then slipped back outside.

Opening the laptop and turning it on, Bud keyed in the words, *Hayden Survey explorer Nathaniel Langford.* A number of sites came up, and he clicked on the first.

Nathaniel Pitt Langford (1832–1911) was an American explorer, business-man, and historian who played an important role in the early years of the Montana gold fields, territorial government, and the creation of Yellowstone National Park.

Bud now keyed in *first ascent Grand Teton.* He read:

In 1898, federal surveyor William Owen, Reverend Spalding, and Jackson Hole ranchers Frank Petersen and John Shive made an ascent of the Grand Teton by what is now called the Owen-Spalding Route.

The Rocky Mountain Alpine Club sponsored the climb, but when the news was published in the New York Herald, Nathaniel P. Langford claimed to have reached the summit on July 29, 1872 with James Steven-son. Their account of the climb was published in 1893 in Scribner's Magazine.

Many find that their description and sketches match the summit of the Enclosure on a side peak of the Grand Teton, not the Grand itself. The Enclosure is a rock structure of unknown origin.

It is not possible to discount or prove Langford's claim, but Owen's is an established fact. But a new claimant appeared in a letter to Owen dated April 3, 1899, where Captain Charles Kieffer of the U.S. Army claimed that he, Private Logan Newell, and a third man, probably Private John Rhyan, climbed the peak on September 10, 1893.

Kieffer was stationed at Fort Yellowstone during the summer of 1893 and probably did have the opportunity to make the ascent. A drawing done by Kieffer shows his route to have been the Exum Ridge, a technically diffi-cult route named for Glenn Exum's solo ascent in 1931. Owen kept the letter secret and it came to light only when it was uncovered in 1959 in the Owen papers at the University of Wyoming American Heritage Center.

Bud closed the laptop and kicked back, finishing his coffee. It seemed obvious that Marty Langford was a descendent of Nathaniel P. Langford, but was Jamie McKenzie somehow a descendent of one of the Owens-Spalding group and thereby carrying on the controversy? Hadn't Winnie said it was an old feud that went back several generations in Jamie and Marty's families?

Had Marty stolen the plaque from the top of the Grand? Was that why Jamie, possibly assuming Winnie had the plaque, had broken into her bus and yet not taken anything? Was that what he'd been looking for? And where did Winnie get it? Did she somehow have access to Marty's stuff, now that he was dead?

Bud decided it was time to ask Winnie about all this, and since the sun was now rising over the Tetons, he knew everyone would soon be getting up. There had been talk the previous evening about going into Driggs for breakfast, so hopefully Winnie would join them, and he could talk to her afterwards in private.

But in the meantime, he knew he had a couple of hours before that would happen, as it was still early, and Bud had a plan—he needed to get back out to the campground now that it was getting light and see if he could find any clues as to what had happened the previous night with Winnie.

He slipped back into the kitchen and poured more instant coffee into his thermos, grabbed a handful of biscuits for Lindie, grabbed some oatmeal cookies, then left a quick note saying where he'd gone.

He then quietly tiptoed into the bedroom where Wilma Jean and the boys were still sleeping, took his Ruger and its holster from the nightstand drawer, grabbed his clothes and hiking boots, then quietly closed the door, managing to not wake even the dogs, marveling at their failure as guard dogs.

He changed from his PJs in the living room, then back outside, he and Lindie jumped into the FJ and headed for Teton Canyon, just as the sun rose over the ramparts of the Middle Teton, lighting up the spires and jagged heights with what looked like gold foil.

He was soon in the canyon, the deep forest still casting shadows where the sun hadn't yet reached. It was the perfect time of day to photograph wildlife, and just as he realized he'd forgotten his camera, a small herd of deer bolted across the road in front of him.

Slowing, he thought again of the wolf he'd seen the previous night, then of the bear that had been raiding camps, resulting in the campground being closed. He hoped it was still deep asleep in some forest thicket.

Reaching the chain across the gate, he got out and opened it, then drove through. He'd leave it open, as he didn't intend to take much time in the campground, but instead, something made him stop and replace it.

Winnie's small canvas tent was still there, and Bud started to pull up next to it in order to throw it into the FJ, but his intuition said to instead park behind the nearby cinder-block bathroom, out of sight.

As he got out and came around the small building, he spotted vehicle lights coming into the campground. Slipping back behind the bathroom, he put Lindie back into the FJ, then watched from around the corner.

A pickup stopped by Winnie's tent and two figures got out, each carrying a backpack. Stopping by the tent, he could barely hear a voice say, "What happened to Winnie's VW?"

A second voice replied, "You saw the sign. They closed the campground again because of bears, and she left. But we can go ahead and use her tent. She won't care. But let's hurry, as I don't want to hang around here if there is a bear."

"What about the rest of the stuff?" The first voice asked.

"We'll drop it off later and let her know it's here."

The two zipped the canvas tent open, and Bud could see them put the packs inside. They closed the tent back up, then got back into the truck and were soon gone.

Bud waited for a moment, wanting to make sure the pair wasn't coming back, then went over to the tent, unzipping it and ducking inside. He wasn't much for getting into other people's stuff, but he had a hunch the packs might hold something of interest.

The first pack held a cotton bag, and he pulled out something that felt like a small rock. Holding it to the light, he could see it was a piece of shale, and a closer inspection revealed a fossil embedded in it.

Looking closer, he could see that the bag contained more small pieces of shale. He opened the second pack to find more of the same. He removed several of the pieces and stuck them in his jacket pocket, then went back to the opposite side of the bathroom, hesitating, not sure whether to take the tent down or not since it now held the packs.

He went back to the tent, and looking around closely, he could see a set of distinctive tracks that looked vaguely familiar, with well-defined arrows on the soles and the word *Vibram*. He decided to leave the tent up, and he and Lindie were soon on their way back to the Teewinot Cafe.

It took awhile, but just as he pulled into the drive, he finally remembered where he'd seen those kind of tracks before—it was on the flanks of Teewinot, and they'd belonged to Ranger Jamie McKenzie!

25

Bud and Shorty sat on the back deck of the Teewinot Cafe, Shorty throwing a ball to Lindie while Bud tried to get Hoppie and Pierre to let go of a sock they were playing tug of war with.

"That sock is one Wilma Jean gave me for my birthday, and it's kind of special," Bud noted, the boys refusing to give it up, growling and tugging on it. "It has a Yeti on it. I think that's why they like it so much."

"Where's the mate?" Shorty asked.

"Here on my other foot," Bud replied. "I'm still recovering from the blisters I got when we first came up here, and I was putting a bandaid on when they stole my sock, the rascals."

"Your socks kind of match your PJs," Shorty grinned. "Which, by the way, made us all think something weird had happened to you, the way they were just lying there on the living room floor. Good thing you left a note, as Wilma Jean was about to call some UFO investigators. Breakfast was good, but what's on the schedule for the rest of the day?"

"I have no idea," Bud replied. "The gang's inside figuring it out right now. You know, we've been here awhile, Shorty, and I've really enjoyed it, but everyone's talking about going home before long. What's going on with your contract with the park? When are you leaving?"

"So far, I haven't accomplished a darn thing, Bud, so I'm not sure Cam even needs my services anymore. I'm not privy to what's going on with the investigation of the ranger's death, and Cam was still wanting to hike to Fossil Mountain, but now that you've figured out the fossils are fake, I really don't see a need to."

"I don't know, maybe we should go anyway," Bud replied. "But Shorty, what goes into the making of a fossil—a real one, I mean?"

"Do you want the short version or the long one?"

"I don't know, what's the difference?"

"Only a few hundred million years, maybe more, maybe less, depending."

"Hows about the Shorty version."

Shorty laughed, then said, "You know, I've always wanted to ask you something. If Sherlock Holmes were a geologist, what would his most famous line be?"

"I have no idea."

"Sedimentary, my dear Watstone."

Bud groaned as Shorty continued. "Sorry. Anyway, a fossil is a preserved lifeform from a past geologic time. The data recorded by fossils is called the fossil record and is how we geologists and paleontologists get our knowledge about the history of life on Earth."

Sensing Shorty was about to switch into his long-winded professorial mode, Bud said, "I know you used to teach at Stanford, but I just want the basics, like in Fossilology 101. How are they formed?"

"OK, I'll try to keep it simple. Only a small fraction of ancient organisms are preserved as fossils, and those typically have a calcareous skeleton or shell, such as brachiopods and corals, or bones with calcium phosphate, like dinosaurs. The hard parts of organisms that become buried in sediment may have their pores filled with solutions of calcium carbonate or other mineral salts which harden and fossilize the remains, which is called permineralization. Sometimes you have mineralization, which is a total replacement of the original skeletal material by other mineral matter. There are other ways to fossilize something, but those are the two main ones."

"I thought you were going to keep it simple," Bud replied.

"Believe me, I am," Shorty replied. "It gets complicated fast."

"What conditions need to exist for all this to happen?" Bud asked.

"Well, the majority of fossils are preserved in a marine environment, as anaerobic conditions at the bottom of bodies of water are especially good for preserving fine details, and it helps not having other critters there to destroy the remains. But in general, two conditions must be met—rapid burial to retard decomposition, and possession of hard parts capable of being fossilized."

"Are the soft parts ever fossilized?" Bud asked.

"Very rarely," Shorty replied. "That's what makes the Burgess Shale so valuable, as all the soft parts were preserved—I mean everything, even tiny antennae and legs and such. It's like a snapshot of the critter. About the only time you really see full-body preservation is with the embedding of insects in amber and the preservation of the carcasses of Pleistocene mammoths in glacier ice. You do get the preservations of insects and leaves and such with carbonization, where such parts are flattened between two layers of rock. The plant or insect will be preserved in a carbon film that occurs on one layer of rock while an impression of that part occurs on the other layer of the rock, like mirror images. The Eocene has lots of examples of that in places like the Green River Formation."

Bud took out his yoyo and practiced while Shorty continued, but soon put it down, caught up in what he was saying.

"People wonder why fossils are important, but they can tell us a great deal about life on Earth and how it evolved. The study of the fossil record lets us determine relative ages of the strata in which they occur, as well as information about the climate and environment where they were deposited, as well as how tectonic plates have moved things. For example, coral fossils tell us the area was once warm and tropical, and we can determine plate movements through such things. These are all reasons scientists are against nonscientific collecting and the commercial selling of fossils. We lose invaluable information."

"So," Bud said slowly, reaching into his pocket. "I take it you wouldn't condone selling stuff like this?" He held up one of the fossils he'd taken from Winnie's tent.

Shorty took it, and after examining it, said, "Holy smokes, Bud! There's no question that this is the real deal. Where did you get it?"

After Bud told him, Shorty said, "Well, I'm now revising my statement about not needing to go to Fossil Mountain—do you think that's where these came from? Maybe the two figures Howie saw digging? This is really exciting—you say they had two backpacks full? Bud, this could be another lagerstätte."

"What's that?" Bud asked.

"It's German for 'storage place' and refers to a site of exceptional fossilization where soft tissue preservation and other highly detailed remains are found. The Burgess Shale is one, as is the Green River Formation in Wyoming, which I mentioned. Wyoming fossils show exceptional preservation of mostly fish, though there are insects, too, as well as small vertebrates such as lizards, along with birds and small mammals. If this turns out to be another lagerstätte, it could be an invaluable addition to the fossil record. But it appears someone is looting it."

"And maybe the same someones who made the fake fossils, but maybe not."

"The plot thickens," Shorty replied. "And it may all be tied to the ranger's death."

"Or maybe not," Doc added, coming out from the house, carrying his pipe. "Or maybe I have no idea what either of you are talking about. But I want to know if the collective noun for geologists is a *conglomerate* of geologists or a *formation* of geologists? Which is it?"

Shorty laughed. "How about a *melange* of geologists? But that's probably over your head, Doc, since you haven't studied the accretion of exotic terranes. To put it simply, melanges are typically a jumble of rocks of various types."

"Kind of like geologists," Doc replied. "A jumble of various types. But Shorty, I don't think you even know the meaning of simple. Everything you say is typically way over my head. But the gals sent me out here to see if anyone wants to go to some hot springs over in Swan Valley. We can go soak and relax."

"You mean over on the other side of the Big Hole Mountains?" Bud asked.

Doc replied, "They said it's less than an hour's drive, so that's not too bad. They were talking about going to Yellowstone, which is too much driving in one day for me. But I'm going, as is Howie. How about you two? We can take the dogs and let them sleep in the car while we're soaking. There are lots of places to let them out on the way over and back. Wilma Jean wants me to talk you into it, and you, too, Shorty. You need a break."

"Has anyone seen Winnie?" Bud asked. "I may need to take her into town to get a new window."

"I forgot," Doc said. "She asked me to tell you that she already had it scheduled and wouldn't be back until this evening. She wants to stay in the drive again, and I told her it was fine."

"We need to leave her the key code so she can come on inside," Shorty said. "Does anyone have her phone number?"

"I'm not sure she even has a phone," Doc replied. "Does this mean you're coming? The gals brought their swimsuits—as usual, they're prepared for anything fun. But we're going to stop in town and see if we can find some swim trunks for the rest of us."

"Sure, why not? I could use a break, like you said," Shorty replied. "And Bud, too. He's been losing sleep over these dang fossils. Let's all go have some fun. Maybe we'll see some buffalo—or bison."

They all went inside, though Bud was wishing he could talk to Winnie, but he wasn't even really sure what he would ask her at this point.

Back in the house, Lindie appeared to be chewing something, and Wilma Jean asked, "What in the world does she have, Bud?"

"Drop it!" Bud commanded, then picking up what Lindie had

been chewing, said with chagrin, "It's my yoyo! Bad doggie! Now it's full of chew marks."

"Does it still work?" Howie asked.

Trying to deploy the yoyo, Bud said, "I don't think so, but I'll have to wait until it dries out. The string's all soggy."

"Such are the woes of the yoyo pro," Doc laughed. "But let's get ready to go."

26

"Sheriff, I'm not the type to go stew in hot water—I don't even like to take baths," Howie moaned, he and Bud back outside, waiting for everyone to go to the hot springs.

"Me, neither, Howie. I'm more a shower kind of guy. But how do we get out of this one without making our wives mad?"

"Well, we could come up with some kind of outrageous excuse, or we could just be honest," Howie replied. "I kind of like the outrageous excuse thing better, but I can't think of one."

"We could say we need to go moose hunting so we have something for dinner tonight," Bud offered.

"Hey, Bud, that's not a bad idea! If I came up with something really delicious for dinner, something that takes a long time to make, maybe we could get away with not going."

"That might work for you, but what about me?"

"It has to be something I need help with. Like maybe something that requires a big pit to cook it in, that kind of thing."

"A pit or a pot?"

"A pit."

"Well, I'm not real big on pig roasts," Bud replied. "I always feel bad for the pig."

"No, Sheriff, not that!" Howie said. "Just something that takes a long time."

"Tamales? Deviled eggs? Macaroons?"

"I can tell you're not a cook."

"Beef wellington? Doesn't that take a lot of work? Or hows about ravioli? Or what if I dug a pizza pit?"

Now coming out the door, Wilma Jean asked, "What's a pizza pit?"

"Hon," Bud said. "Howie and I want to prepare the dinner of a lifetime for you guys. It's going to take us all day, so we won't be able to go to the hot springs."

"What in the world are you going to make that takes all day?" She asked incredulously.

Howie replied, "Raspberry cheesecake with homemade ice cream, challah, beef wellington, baked Alaska, tiramisu, gourmet soup, those kinds of things."

Wilma Jean laughed. "Sounds like you're starting a business. You could call it the Teewinot Cafe."

"It fits," Bud replied lamely.

Maureen, now also on the front porch, said, "You guys are too transparent—I knew you'd weasel out of going some way or another. At least Doc and Shorty actually want to go. But if you stay, we're going to hold you to making dinner."

"That's exactly what we were offering to do," Howie replied. "And not just any old dinner, something really yummy and gourmet."

"We'll be back around dark," Maureen replied. "And we'll be hungry."

"It's OK," Wilma Jean added. "I kind of didn't want to leave the dogs in the car while we soaked. This will be better for them."

Bud sighed as the gang drove off, glad to not be going. He much preferred hanging around with Howie and the dogs.

"Let's go get some lunch," Howie suggested. "There's a place that looks pretty good not too far from the grocery store. We can have lunch, then get stuff for dinner and take it back to the house, and then we'll have all day to do whatever we want."

They were soon in a small unassuming restaurant called the

Royal Magpie, sitting in the back booth and studying the menu, which Bud thought was much more impressive than the cafe itself, which seemed a little dark.

"I don't even know what a lot of this stuff is, Howie," Bud said. "What are Parmesan Truffle Fries?"

"Fries cooked in white truffle oil and sprinkled with black truffle salt, Bud," Howie replied. "Everyone knows that, plus it says so right on the menu. And look, they have buffalo burgers—and you can get a Colossal Idaho Spud, which looks to just be a baked potato."

The server took their order, and as they waited, a couple came in and headed for the booth next to them. As they came closer, Bud could see that it was Winnie and Jamie! Bud quickly held his menu in front of his face, though the place was dark enough he wasn't sure they would notice him anyway.

He nodded to Howie to be quiet. They could clearly hear them talking, and after they'd ordered, Winnie said, "That was really nice of you to stop by and offer to pay for a new window for the bus, then take me out to eat."

Jamie replied, "I'm glad I saw you parked at the old cafe. Do you know people there?"

"They're some nice tourists who offered to let me sleep in their driveway," Winnie replied. "I was pretty shook up and didn't want to stay at the campground."

"Another bear scare?" Jamie asked. "I'm glad you got the window installed so quickly. I don't mind paying for it. We go way back, Winnie, and I know you don't have a ton of money."

Winnie replied, "You shouldn't mind, Jamie."

"Why do you say that?"

"Because you're the one that broke it in the first place."

"Why would you say that?" Jamie repeated in surprise.

"Look, I heard you talking. I recognized your voice. Who was with you?"

Jamie sighed. "Nobody you know. OK, my nephew. We'd had a couple of beers, and in his defense, I told him I was trying to get something that had been stolen from me, which was true. Winnie,

I'm sorry. It was an exercise in extremely poor judgment. After I found out Marty was dead I knew you had the plaque."

"Why would you think that? Did you go ask at his house?"

Jamie answered, "Yes. His daughter was cleaning everything out, and she said she gave it to you."

"Marty wanted me to take it if anything ever happened to him. He didn't want you to have it."

"So you're saying you still have it?" Jamie asked, then pleaded, "Please, Winnie let me have it back. You have no idea what that means to my family. My great-grandmother, Owen's wife, had that plaque made. It means more than you could ever imagine."

Winnie snorted. "That plaque was a lie. Marty's great grandfather claimed the Grand before yours did by several years. And you're lucky I don't press charges against you and your nephew."

"I appreciate it, but Winnie, we've had this argument a million times—you and me and Marty. His great-grandfather only made it to the Enclosure."

Winnie replied, "That's where he describes stopping, but he went on to the summit. Why wouldn't he, when he was so close? And he told his wife, Marty's great-grandmother, that he did."

"There's absolutely no proof that he climbed the Grand, Winnie," Jamie replied. "The Enclosure's on a side peak. Can I get the plaque back? Now that Marty's gone, the argument's over."

The server brought Bud and Howie's lunch, and they ate silently, still listening in on Winnie and Jamie's conversation.

"What are you going to do with the plaque?" Winnie asked. "Put it back up on the Grand? And you know there's evidence that someone else climbed it even before your and Marty's families did—that army lieutenant or whatever he was."

"That's just speculation," Jamie said. "He had no proof of any kind. Nor did Marty's great-grandfather. Mine did. The climb was organized by the Rocky Mountain Alpine Club and followed closely, complete with photographs."

"And you thought it was OK to break into my VW looking for the plaque, scaring me to death?"

"I thought you slept in the tent," Jamie replied. "I had no idea you were in the VW. I didn't mean to break the window. I was trying to jimmy the lock and the window fell into the frame."

Winnie replied, "But after I jumped out, you chased me all the way up Fred's Mountain. You totally terrorized me, Jamie, and I'm still not over it. The only reason I'm having lunch with you is because I want to find out what you know about Marty."

"Winnie, I didn't chase you up the mountain."

"Somebody did. But what do you know about Marty's death?"

"I don't know anything. I wasn't even around when it happened. I have proof that I wasn't."

Winnie asked, "Did you know that he put another plaque on Teewinot? His great-grandfather claimed to have climbed that one first, also."

"He put a plaque up there? How do you know that?"

"He told me."

"Have you been up there to see it?" Jamie asked. "Maybe he just made it up. I was up there two weeks ago, and there wasn't a plaque."

"That's because he did it right before he died."

Jamie said, "Another ridiculous claim. The first ascent of Teewinot was in 1929 by Fritiof Fryxell and Phil Smith."

"Is there proof?" Winnie asked.

"I don't know," Jamie replied.

"Anyway, I no longer have your plaque, Jamie."

"Where is it?"

"It's in the bottom of the Teton River. I got sick of it all and decided to get rid of it once and for all."

"Winnie, why would you throw it in the river? Even if you didn't agree with it, it had a lot of historical value. Cam wanted to put it in the park museum."

Winnie replied, "I never want to see that plaque again. Let's just drop the whole thing and let bygones be bygones. Marty's gone. The feud's over. Marty's daughter has no interest in any of it."

"All right, Winnie, but I sure wish you hadn't done that. It belongs in a museum.

"Too late now."

The server brought their food, and they were silent for awhile, eating. Finally, Jamie said, "You know, it's just really tragic what happened to Marty. But you know, Teewinot's famous for rockfall."

Winnie paused, then asked quietly, "Do you think that's what killed him? I heard he was hit on the head and wondered if it was a natural death or if something else happened."

"I really shouldn't talk about it, you know that," Jamie replied. "It's still being investigated as a possible murder, based on some witnesses. That's all I know."

"There were witnesses? How could there be witnesses? Did you talk to them?"

"No, Cam did. But what do you mean, how could there be witnesses?"

Winnie stammered, "I thought he was way out in the backcountry somewhere, with nobody around."

"I thought you knew he was found on Teewinot. But Winnie, let's put the hatchet away."

"Alright. It's not going anywhere, anyway, now that Marty's dead. How're the wife and kids?"

"They're doing fine."

"And Cam and his wife?"

"They're fine. We had dinner with them a few nights ago. Margaret's getting ready to go visit her sister in New England, so we're going to have to find a temporary babysitter for the grands. What are you going to do with the campground closed?"

"It'll open up here in a day or two once the bear moves on or they trap and relocate it. Actually, I'm going to drive on back out there today and see if anything is going on."

Finishing his lunch, Bud was trying to process everything that had been said. The grands? Was Jamie somehow related to Cam? Why else would he refer to his kids as Cam's grandkids? And neither Jamie nor Winnie seemed to know that Shorty had given Cam the plaque. And why would Winnie want to find out what Jamie knew about Marty's death? Did she suspect him of somehow being involved? Had Jamie killed Marty over the feud over who had been the first to climb the Grand Teton? And yet, she didn't seem to be accusing him.

Done with lunch, Bud and Howie ordered coffee, waiting for Winnie and Jamie to leave, not wanting to be seen. They didn't have to wait long, for the pair soon left.

"Well, that was an interesting conversation," Howie said as he and Bud left the cafe.

"It was," Bud replied. "And now I'd like to go out to Teton Canyon and look around some more before Winnie gets out there. We can pick up groceries later, Howie, but let's hurry out there. Last night the people with the packs said something that made me think they had more fossils and were taking them out there."

"You're not waiting on me," Howie replied, jumping into the FJ. "Let's go."

27

"Howie, do you mind not coming over here by the tent? I want to be sure none of these tracks get messed up before I can check them out."

Bud was carefully studying the ground around the tent, hoping to make sense of the tracks from the two figures with the backpacks full of fossils. The packs were still inside, but there was nothing new.

"Sure, Bud," Howie replied, heading over to the other side of Winnie's campsite. "I'll just look around over here and keep an eye out. Didn't you say they were coming back?"

"They said they would bring the rest back," Bud replied. "And I'm just assuming they meant fossils, since that's what they had in their packs. But they apparently haven't been back. There's only one track set that's really legible, and it sure looks like the photo I took of Jamie's tracks up by the grave on Teewinot."

"That sure would be a shame to see him messed up with fossil looting," Howie replied. "Especially in his own park."

"Yeah, and after trying to get us arrested," Bud replied. "Remember how he told me to leave the fossil? Maybe he wanted it for himself." Flashing on Doc's words earlier, he added, "But we can't go making assumptions."

Looking around more, Bud finally said, "Howie, these tracks go over to where you're at. Maybe you should just stay put, sit on a rock or something, while I look around."

Bud followed the tracks, which now seemed to circle where Winnie's bus had been.

"It looks like they went all around the bus, looking at it from every angle, and not very stealthily, I might add. And look, now they go over toward the bathroom."

After following the tracks as best he could, Bud finally said, "Howie, this is the most confusing tracking I've ever tried to do. Now the tracks are going over to where you're at again."

"Maybe I can help..."

"No, stay put. Actually, why don't you go on over to the next camp-site and wait. That way there's no chance you'll contaminate anything. Now there's a set going back over to the tent."

Finally, Bud sat on the same rock Howie had been sitting on. After a few minutes had passed, Howie yelled from the next camp-site, "Bud, there's different tracks over here!"

Bud got up and walked over to where Howie was. There, a new set of tracks proceeded up a small dusty path that looked like it went around the back side of the campground.

"It's a social trail, Howie, and sure enough, they're heading up it."

"What's a social trail?" Howie asked.

"It's one that gets created organically, like the shortest distance between points, as opposed to one that's been planned by a trail builder, like for the Forest Service or something. Let's follow it."

"There are people who plan trails?" Howie asked.

"Yes, most agencies like the Forest Service or BLM have profes-sional trail builders, or they hire it out when they build a new trail. There's a science to creating a trail that doesn't destroy fragile plants or cut through areas important to wildlife, plus you need grades that people can negotiate. And a good trail builder also makes note of the scenery and aesthetics of a place, as well as making the trail inter-esting by going around rock outcrops to nice views and things like that."

"Wow, I had no idea," Howie replied. "I bet social trails don't do all that."

"No, they usually just go from one point to another in the shortest manner. Like this one we're on. It looks like it's going straight up the side of the hill."

"Are you still seeing Jamie's boot prints?" Howie asked.

"Actually, no, but I *am* following someone's prints, but they're much smaller. And here they cut off from the trail. Let's see where they go. They're probably just someone who was staying in the campground, but they look fresh. But it's getting pretty steep and I need to catch my breath for a minute."

Bud sat on a nearby rock as Howie walked ahead, scouting out the trail. He was soon back, saying, "Bud, they go over to that rock outcrop. Maybe they're the tracks of a trail designer after all, trying to make things interesting."

Bud laughed, but it was strained.

"Howie, sit down here and take a little break. I have a confession to make."

"Oh, man, Sheriff, this sounds serious. Are you sure you want to tell me whatever it is you're thinking about? I hope it doesn't have anything to do with our friendship, like I was talking about earlier."

Bud laughed. "No, no, it's nothing like that Howie. But you know me—I've done lots of tracking, have even taken tracking classes and field seminars put on by the Utah Sheriff's Association."

Howie replied, "Oh, I know, Sheriff. You're good at it, too."

"*Was* good at it. Howie, I've made one of the worst mistakes an investigator could make. If you'll recall, I took a photo of the tracks up by the grave on Teewinot, then when Jamie came around, I could see that the tracks matched his boots perfectly. So I just assumed he'd been up there earlier, which I think was a safe assumption, as he was the one handling that case."

Bud paused, and Howie said, "Go ahead, Sheriff."

"Well, when I came out here to Winnie's campsite earlier and saw the two people with the fossils in their packs, I watched them go over to the tent and leave the packs. After they left, I went and got samples from their packs. I then looked around and saw the same footprints as Jamie's, I mean, exactly the same, so I linked them with Jamie, as I knew he'd been here. OK, so we come back out, and I'm looking all around, and I now see his prints all over the place. I was beginning to think he'd come back after I left."

"You just didn't look that closely when you were out here before, Bud, that's all. What's the problem?"

"Howie, hold up your boot so I can see the bottom."

Howie held up his boot.

"Now look at the bottom of mine," Bud said, holding up his boot.

Howie said, "They have the same tread, Bud, and that *Vibram* word. That's because we got the same kind of boots."

Bud replied, "Remember how Georgie, the saleswoman at Wydaho Outdoors, said these boots were very popular with the back-country rangers? Well, Howie, Jamie's wearing the same kind of boots. We have three different sets of boots, all with the same tread. I was tracking myself all this time, and sometimes you. I walked all around that tent earlier. I have no proof that Jamie was ever near it, yet alone that he was one of the fossil guys."

"Wow, Bud, that's one I would've never thought of."

Bud replied, "I should have, as I'm well aware that tracks do not hold water in the courtroom unless they're highly unusual and one of a kind."

Howie asked, "So, if one's going to commit a crime, you should always buy new boots first?"

"Probably wouldn't hurt," Bud replied. "Though there are other clues, such as the kind of dirt on your soles and the wear on the tread and that kind of thing. A good forensic geologist can tell where you've been if the dirt matches."

"So I should wear baggies on the bottom of my boots before I commit a crime?"

"Maybe, but don't forget to take them off. They'll leave pretty distinctive prints—or better yet, throw your boots away. But Howie, sitting here thinking of Jamie makes me wonder—I bet he didn't even know that Marty was dead when we met up with him on Teewinot.

Remember how pale his face went? I assumed it was because he was worried that we knew the grave was where Marty had been buried, and maybe he'd been the one to bury him there. But given what we now know about the feud he had with Marty, it would make more sense that he would react that way if he was worried that someone thought he'd killed Marty."

"He knew Marty was missing, though," Howie said. "And whose grave was it then? And why try to arrest us for Marty's death if he didn't even know he was dead?"

"I don't know," Bud replied. "And yes, Jamie did know Marty was missing, but if he was responsible for Marty's death, he wouldn't have been so surprised when we told him. Howie, I'm beginning to think Jamie had nothing to do with Marty's death. And if he is somehow related to Cam, I think that when Cam found out Marty might have been murdered, he worried about Jamie being involved and that's why he called me off the case. He knew about their feud. I think Cam's a straight shooter, but when family's possibly involved, you tread a little more carefully."

Howie was silent for awhile, then said, "It's too much for my ten-cent brain. But Bud, there's no way we're going to have time to get groceries and make a gourmet dinner for everyone after all this. It's getting late."

"I have a plan for that, Howie."

"Pizza?" Howie asked.

"No, we call in to the Royal Magpie, where we had lunch, and order take-out dinners for everyone."

"It'll cost a fortune, Bud!"

"Maybe, but think of how cheap this trip has been because we can stay at the Teewinot Cafe for free. No lodging costs."

"I'll split it with you—is that OK?"

Bud replied, "Sure, that way it won't be too bad for either of us."

Howie said, "We'll throw out the takeout cartons and make it look like we cooked it. Maureen's always wishing I'd learn some real cooking instead of the drive-in kind of stuff like hamburgers and chili."

"It'll knock her socks off, Howie. They had some pretty gourmet stuff on the menu—top sirloin with portabella mushrooms and blue cheese, mashed potatoes and sautéed vegetables, and chocolate-strawberry crunch cake."

"You remember what was on the menu?"

"Yeah, I'm kind of keyed into stuff like that," Bud laughed.

Howie grinned, but just then Bud grabbed his arm, saying, "Somebody's coming! Quick, get behind these rocks!"

They hid just in time to see two figures hiking up the side trail, and Bud knew it was the same people, coming for the rest of the stuff —stuff that he would bet his last meal on Earth was illegal fossils.

28

"Jill and I hid them in these rocks," a woman's voice said, a voice so close to them that Bud and Howie thought they would soon be discovered. But the voices stopped just before coming around to the back of the rock outcrop where he and Howie hid.

"I can't believe you came back out here last night to hide this," a second woman's voice said. "In the dark with a rogue bear around."

"It took me and Jill a very long day to get all this down yesterday. We were pretty scared someone would see us. We just didn't feel comfortable putting all of it in the tent where someone might find it. But you should see all the fireweed in Darby Canyon! It's everywhere up there! Tall stalks with gorgeous purple flowers. They bloom from the bottom up, and when the last little flower at the top falls off, summer's over."

The first voice sounded familiar, and Bud was pretty sure he knew who the second voice was.

"Well, let's get all this into our packs and head down before someone comes into the campground," said the second voice, who Bud was now pretty sure was Winnie.

"I'm really glad it's closed," the first voice said.

They were silent, and Bud knew they were putting the fossils into their packs. Finally, the first voice said, "They barely fit."

"It's pretty heavy," said the second voice.

"Don't hurt yourself, Winnie," said the first voice. "I can get Jill to come back up if I need to. She gets off work at five."

"I'm OK, but what do you think I should do with all this?" Winnie asked. "I really appreciate you and Jill bringing it all down for me before someone else made off with it."

"Call Jamie. They may be illegal," said the first voice, trailing off, and Bud knew they were heading back down the trail. After he was sure they were gone, he stepped out from behind the rocks.

"That was Winnie and Georgie," Howie said. "What do you think they're doing?"

"I knew Winnie's voice, but I wasn't sure about Georgie's," Bud replied, examining a small cavity in the outcropping where the fossils had been hid. "I have no idea what they're doing, Howie, except hauling fossils out, and they know they're illegal—and they're going to call Jamie. Is he in on all this illegal fossil stuff, or were they going to call him to turn it in?"

"Man, this place is starting to make my head hurt, Sheriff. Maybe it's time to go home."

Bud replied, "I've been thinking about going home myself. I think the gals are starting to worry about things back there, and I don't know how many more days they're good for."

"We can go back anytime, Bud. We have our own transportation. They can come with us or stay a few more days."

"I know, but I'm not really wanting to leave quite yet. If I left now, I'd lie awake at night wondering what was going on up here, even though it's not really my deal. Shorty said he wasn't being of much help to Cam, but Howie, if we can get up to Fossil Mountain and to where you took that photo of people digging, we might be able to figure all this out, which would also help Shorty."

"And Cam," Howie added. "Though I'm wondering if he's not in on it all, too. I mean, if Jamie is, Cam very well could be. Imagine that, the head of a national park."

"Howie, I'm beginning to wonder if Winnie doesn't know more than she's letting on. I mean, when she was talking to Jamie and asked how there could be witnesses? Doesn't that sound like she might be worried about someone having seen Marty murdered? Who would worry about that unless they were also there and maybe even did it?"

"Winnie? She doesn't strike me as the type at all, Bud. Not a bit," Howie replied.

Bud said, "No one ever knows what someone's truly capable of until their back's up against the wall. Remember the case of that older woman out in California in the 1980s? She wore chiffon dresses, had gray hair and cats, and ran a small boarding house. She insisted everyone call her grandma. But she was actually a serial killer who killed her tenants and kept their Social Security checks. Because she took in the homeless, nobody noticed until a social worker investigated."

"Wow, Bud, that's terrible. Do you think Winnie is going around killing rangers in national parks?"

Bud groaned as Howie added, "Just kidding. But I'll keep an eye on her, just in case."

They headed back down the trail, and as they came to the campground, they could see Winnie's VW bus in her spot with a pickup parked next to it, and Winnie talking to a short gray-haired man.

As they stopped, Howie whispered, "Bud, that's Parker Watson!"

They soon heard the man yelling, then he got into the pickup, slammed the door and peeled out.

"He's sure mad about something," Howie said.

Bud replied, "Maybe we should wait here for a minute, just in case Winnie's mad, too."

"Yeah, we wouldn't want her to take it out on us, especially if she's a serial killer," Howie said. "Actually, she might not qualify as one until after she gets done with us."

Bud replied, "Howie, don't be silly. Let's go on over there and see what she's doing. We need to get back to the cafe soon anyway, it's getting late."

"The Teewinot Cafe?"

"No, the Royal Magpie."

"Oh, jeez, I forgot all about dinner, which isn't like me when I'm the one making it."

"It's like setting an alarm clock—you know you can forget about having to wake up 'cause the alarm will make sure you do."

"I don't get it," Howie said.

"You know that I'll never forget about dinner, so you can relax and forget about it," Bud replied.

"Oh, I got it now," Howie grinned.

They were soon at Winnie's VW, and Bud called out, "Hello the camp! You in there, Winnie? It's Bud and Howie."

Winnie stuck her head out as Bijou jumped out, his lead just long enough to dive under the bus, which he did upon seeing the pair.

"Bud, Howie! How long have you been here?"

Bud, sensing she was worried that they'd overheard her conversation with Parker, said, "We just got here. We want to invite you to dinner. You are staying in the drive again tonight, right?"

"Where's your FJ?" She asked.

"It's over behind the bathroom. Glad to see you got your window fixed."

"I was lucky they could take it right in. I'd love to have dinner. What time?"

"Well," Bud replied. "Everyone went over to the hot springs in Swan Valley, and they should be back in an hour or two. But you can come anytime."

"Would it be possible to do some laundry there?" Winnie asked. She then added, "I don't know if you noticed, but that scumbag Parker Watson was just here. He wanted me to sell him Marty's gold claim. I told him to get lost."

"It's yours now?" Howie asked.

"He left it to me. His daughter told me a few days ago. I have no idea how Parker found out it's now mine, though he probably just figured that's what Marty would do. That guy Parker's done more damage to this valley than anyone I know."

Bud wasn't sure what to say, so he just stood, silent.

"Bijou, get in here," Winnie said, gently tugging on the cat's lead. "When I first came here, I took up cross-country skiing, and you could ski about any of these big meadows around town and up towards the canyon here, the farmers didn't care. Marty moved here and helped pioneer a lot of runs that are now classics—for example, the Do It Chutes up on Teton Pass, which are a pair of avalanche chutes, the Casino Bowl, also on the pass, and Super Bowl. I was nowhere in his league, but we did ski a lot of the gentler stuff together and had a blast. We loved it here, and there were a number of us who hated what was happening to Jackson. We had something quieter and more affordable here, but with even better snowfall and access. We have backcountry here that spans 50 miles along what was once the untouched west slope of the Tetons."

She picked up Bijou, holding him close, then continued.

"In the meantime, people like Parker had discovered Jackson and Jackson Hole, but they pretty much left us alone over here on the west side. Then Parker and his buddies discovered we had cheap land over here that was only minutes from Grand Targhee and Teton Pass, as well as having what's called an orographic lift that produces more than 500 inches of light, dry snow every year. They saw it for what is was—paradise—powder skiing that's unrivaled anywhere else in the world with unbelievable views. They knew they could monetize it, and they've been doing so ever since. And Parker's the worst of the bunch—he'll try to make money off anything, and the easier, the better. He's a watered-down human who thinks adventure is looking at a forest from your car window. I told him he should become a bed tester, and he drove off in a huff. I would never sell him anything, except he's probably dumb enough to buy my old bus here for ten times what it's worth—actually, I guess I *would* sell it to him for that."

Neither Bud nor Howie knew what to say, and there was an awkward silence for a moment until Howie finally asked, "You OK with sirloin steak?"

Winnie replied, "Of course. I'll follow you guys back after we take down my tent. I'm surprised the bears haven't taken it down for me."

29

Bud casually studied Winnie over dinner, trying to figure out if she had the temperament to possibly have killed her ex-husband, Marty.

She seemed intelligent and congenial enough, but he knew murderers couldn't be stereotyped by personality. In fact, he'd read that, even though one would associate murderers with what psychiatrists called the dark traits of psychopathic behavior, studies had found that homicide was committed by people of all personality types.

Winnie seemed to be enjoying herself and at one point had even complimented the "chefs" on a delicious dinner, winking at Bud as she asked if they'd gotten the recipe for the chocolate-strawberry crunch cake from the Royal Magpie.

After dinner, they all went out onto the back porch, where Bud tossed biscuits to the dogs in a game of catch.

"How was the hot springs?" Howie asked.

"It was great," Doc replied. "They gave me and Shorty our own private pool."

Millie laughed, then said, "It was the kiddie pool. You were ostracized and didn't even know it."

"All I did was ask if we could smoke cigars while soaking," Doc replied. "And they kicked us out and pretended they didn't? Outrageous."

"At least they let us smoke there," Shorty laughed. "I smoke a cigar about twice a year, only on special occasions."

"What was the occasion?" Maureen asked.

"Being able to smoke a cigar while actually having one," Shorty replied.

Winnie said, "This reminds me of when this place was a cafe. Marty and I used to eat here all the time." She was quiet for awhile, as if thinking back, then continued. "Shorty, Bud said you were a geologist. Do you know much about the Tetons?"

"The basics," Shorty replied. "What are you wanting to know?"

"Well, weren't they pretty much created from earthquakes? How does that work?"

Shorty replied, "Yes, the 40-mile long Teton Fault is responsible for the uplift. If you're on the Jackson side, you can see the fault scarp right at timberline. Every two- or three-thousand years or so a 7.0 or bigger earthquake shakes everything up, pushing the mountains higher and dropping the valley lower. The last major earthquake was more than 5,000 years ago, so it's overdue."

"I'd heard it was overdue," Winnie replied. "It makes me think of all the big trophy houses in Jackson, the timberframe and log houses and such. I wonder how they would hold up to a big earthquake."

"Driggs and Alta would be affected, too," Doc said. "The whole region would be a big mess—except you, Winnie. Your VW might rock and roll for awhile, but you'd be OK."

"Unless the canyon walls started coming down," Shorty replied. "Which they very well might, or at least some big rocks."

"I'd hate to be climbing something like the Grand Teton," Maureen added.

Winnie replied, "Teewinot lost some of its top in 1934, but I don't know if it was from an earthquake. If so, it was a small more local one."

"No kidding?" Howie asked.

"Yes, before that, the ascent was much more difficult than it is now. The upper part of the mountain fell, and debris tumbled down all summer. No one was able to climb it that year. Falling rock piled up below the slope on the south summit ridge, and the steep walls and slabs no longer existed."

"Wow, that's crazy," Howie said. "It's amazing no one was killed."

"Rockfall has killed a number of people in the Tetons," Winnie added. "They're a very dangerous place."

Bud again studied Winnie. She'd mentioned rockfall when having lunch with Jamie—was there something she knew about Marty's death that she wasn't sharing? Thinking back to what Cam had told Shorty about someone hearing a booming sound before Marty disappeared, he asked, "Would rockfall cause a booming sound?"

Shorty replied, "Probably not. It typically sounds more like a rifle shot, then you hear the rocks coming down in an avalanche, but that wouldn't make a booming sound."

"What could it be, then?" Bud asked.

"Well," Shorty replied. "The world's a noisy place—sonic booms, meteor explosions, thunder—but it's even more so in earthquake zones. You can get shallow earthquakes, which are more common than one might think. Yellowstone has thousands every year. Earthquakes make a lot of noise if you're near the epicenter, as the energy released from the subsurface is noisy when transmitted into the air. Shallow earthquakes are often only noticeable from their booming sound."

Winnie replied, "So, these booming sounds people report in the Tetons are actually earthquakes? And they can then be followed by rockfall?"

"Have you ever heard one?" Bud asked.

Seeming troubled for a moment, she replied, "Maybe, once."

Shorty added, "A sound like distant thunder or booming is called a brontide, and it's well-known that many have seismic origins. You could easily hear a brontide followed by the sound of rockfall. I've read that earthquakes of magnitude 3.0 to 4.0 typically create loud booms. Anything above that is often reported to have a roaring sound."

"This is all very interesting," Maureen said. "But I'm going to fire up the gas firepit. Does anyone want smores?"

They were soon all sitting around the firepit, roasting marshmallows for smores, laughing and enjoying themselves. Soon, Shorty pulled his camp chair over next to Winnie's, saying, "Not to beat it to death, Winnie, but there is one more possible source in the Tetons for booming sounds, which is the result of its karst topography."

"What's that?" She asked.

"Well," Shorty explained. "The Tetons have some of the oldest rocks in North America, with 2.7 billion-year-old metamorphic gneiss making up much of the range. These rocks were pushed to the surface by the numerous big earthquakes and are what you see on top of many of the big peaks like the Grand Teton, Middle Teton, Mount Owen, and Teewinot."

He paused, thinking, then added, "Not to make this too complicated, but these old layers were pushed up through younger layers of sedimentary limestone, shale, and dolomite, which are visible on the southern extent of the range—where we are, pretty much—in places like Fossil Mountain. These are thick layers—the Madison Limestone, the Darby Formation, the Bighorn Dolomite, and the Gallatin Limestone. They were formed in marine environments and are famous for containing a variety of fossils, including things like crinoids, trilobites, stromatolites, corals, and shells of other organisms. Layers like this are referred to as karst topography, and as we all know, limestone is easily dissolved by water. Karst environments are famous for underground voids—you've heard of Carlsbad Caverns, I'm sure. When you have big rains and storm events, these can send huge volumes of water at high velocity through these voids, sometimes moving debris with it, and this activity is associated with booming sounds."

"So, is that why we have caves like Ice Cave and Darby Cave?" Howie asked.

"Exactly, and I'd still like to hike over to see them," Shorty replied. "What happened to our plan to hike to Fossil Mountain?"

"It was put on hold because of a 3D printer," Bud said. "But has since been revived."

Bud noted that Winnie seemed disturbed, but tried to hide it. She asked, "Fossil Mountain? You're going up there?"

Bud stood, saying, "There's someone at the door. I'll get it."

Winnie also stood. "I need to go finish my laundry."

Opening the front door, Bud was greeted by a sheriff's deputy.

"We have a noise complaint from a neighbor," the man said. "They said you're yelling and hollering and making a ruckus."

Bud was shocked. "We actually have been really quiet, officer. Was it someone from the subdivision next door?"

"I'm not at liberty to say who," the man replied. "I'm just going to ask that you tone it down."

"Not a problem, officer," Bud said. "I'll go talk to everyone."

As the deputy left, Bud noted Winnie peeking around the corner.

"That's Gus," she said. "He's actually an OK guy. Why would anyone call in a noise complaint? We were being really quiet."

"I think I know who it was, Winnie, and it had nothing to do with noise. She just hates that there's a resort rental nearby."

"Oh, you must mean Jessica Barry," Winnie said. "If there's anything going on out in this neck of the woods, you can guarantee she's involved. Her husband, Mason, is actually a decent guy. He spends a lot of time working with the kids at the Teton Science Center. He makes tons of toys and models for them."

"He makes toys?" Bud asked. "Is he a woodworker or something?"

"He has the only 3d printer in the area. He makes stuff out of plastic or whatever they use. But if you guys go to Fossil Mountain, be careful."

"Why?" Bud asked.

Winnie shrugged her shoulders, then said, "People looking for fossils. But I need to go check on Bijou. Thanks for dinner."

With that, she was out the door heading for her VW bus, leaving

Bud even more certain that Mason was the one responsible for the fake fossils, yet wondering why Winnie would tell them to be careful if she herself was the illegal fossil hunter.

30

Bud pulled up in front of the Teton Science Center, a large square building in the center of Driggs surrounded by a plaza with decorative plants and benches along with displays about the Tetons, from the flora and fauna to the geology and weather.

He and Shorty and Howie got out of the FJ and slowly walked around, studying the displays, though Bud's heart wasn't in it, and he suspected Howie's wasn't either, as interesting as it all was.

They'd been informed the previous night that the gals had decided to go home, and Doc had finally decided it would be best to go with them, though Bud could tell he wanted to stay. Maureen was missing Baby Malcolm, and Wilma Jean was worried about things back home, and they'd decided it was time to return.

Since Millie and Doc were riding with them, they'd decided to go back, too, since Bud's FJ wouldn't be able to accommodate them for the trip back. Shorty had indicated his job was almost finished and so the odds were good he'd be riding back with Bud and Howie. Bud wasn't sure when they themselves would be returning, but he suspected it wouldn't be much longer, the way things were going with the fossil department.

Bud knew Howie preferred to go back with the gang, but he'd told

Bud he wanted to see everything through, though Bud wasn't sure what that everything referred to—Marty's death or the source of the fossils, both the real ones and the fake ones.

Bud stopped to admire a tall yellow stand of some kind of decorative grass that swayed in the breeze, wondering if something similar would look nice back at the bungalow in Green River, and it was then that it hit him—that old lonesome feeling he'd felt before when far away from home.

He'd never felt it while in civilization and accompanied by friends, as it usually hit when he was in the backcountry and feeling insignificant. He knew he was already missing Wilma Jean and the boys, though it hadn't been more than an hour since they'd left. Fortunately, Lindie had stayed with him, even though he'd debated about sending her back, as he knew she would miss Hoppie and Pierre.

He realized Howie and Shorty were now going inside the building, Howie asking if he was coming, so he jumped up and followed them inside, where they wandered around.

As they stood looking at a display on the tectonic forces that had built the Tetons, Howie said, "You sure look mournful, Sheriff. Do I look like that?"

Bud laughed. "A little, Howie. I guess I need to pull myself together, eh? I'm already missing everyone, and we didn't even expect them to come up here, so we got to see them more than we might have."

"Yeah," Howie replied. "The one I really miss is little Mal. I bet he's grown a foot or two since I've seen him."

"We've only been up here a little over a week, Howie," Bud replied.

"OK, a few inches," Howie said. "But you know, I decided it was important to stay here with you. I wouldn't want to abandon my good buddy."

"That's nice, Howie," Bud grinned. "Especially since they didn't have room for you."

"Hey, guys, come over here," Shorty called out from across the room. "Fossils!"

As they stood looking at a nice display of petrified wood and fossilized ferns, a woman came up and said, "Good day, gentlemen. I'm Jessica, today's docent for the museum. Be sure to let me know if you have any questions."

She paused, looking at them, then added sarcastically, "Don't I know you from somewhere?"

Shorty, not realizing she was their crotchety neighbor, asked, "Are there more fossil displays?"

Bud figured she must've decided to just ignore everything as she replied, "Yes, come this way," then led them to another display, which had a long and detailed explanation as to how fossils were formed. It also had a large bucket that appeared to be full of fossils with a sign that read, *Free: One Each, Please.*

Bud took a small fossil from the bucket and could immediately see it was an Hallucigenia, identical to the one in the sugar bowl at the house. Howie picked up an Opabinia as Shorty asked, "Are these real?"

Jessica replied, "No, they're made with a 3D printer and are exact replicas."

"Who made them?" Bud asked.

"My husband," Jessica replied proudly. "He's on the Board of Directors and makes all kinds of stuff for the museum. We give tons of these away to help people become more aware of the scientific value of such things. He donates them to the school and various organizations."

"Would he have given some to Parker Watson?" Bud asked.

"I don't know who that is," Jessica replied. "But like I said, he donates them to promote science. He's also a glider pilot if you'd like to take a ride while you're here."

"I've read that you can build a house with 3D printers—can he make mounted heads?" Bud asked.

"I'm sorry, what kind of mounted heads?" Jessica asked.

"The kind you hang on your walls."

"Oh, I get it—like you saw the other evening when you were at our house. No, unfortunately he didn't make those. I wish he could, because then he'd quit shooting everything. He fancies himself a trophy hunter. It's basically the only thing he and I argue about, though I probably shouldn't mention it."

Bud asked, "Where does he hunt? Does he go to Africa or something?"

"No, he stays mostly in Idaho and Wyoming—elk, pronghorn, deer, animals like that."

"So I take it you eat a lot of venison and elk, then," Bud replied. "I grew up on venison, and you have to know how to prepare wild meat properly or it's too gamey tasting."

Jessica replied, "Oh, he knows I would never cook it if he brought it home, so he donates it to the food bank."

Howie, suspecting that Bud's questions were more than just idle conversation, asked, "When is hunting season here, anyway?"

Jessica, now distracted by more people coming in, answered, "I don't know. I think there are various seasons, and it's probably elk season right now, as he just brought home a big elk head. But excuse me, I need to go introduce myself to these new people and see if they need anything."

"Thanks for the information," Bud said as she turned to go. "And we'll try to keep it down next time we have a wild party."

A look of irritation flashed across her face, then she was gone.

They each stuck a fossil in their pockets and went back out to the plaza, where Howie said, "Sheriff, these are exactly like the fossils back at the Teewinot Cafe. Don't you agree, Shorty?"

"They do look the same. We'll know for sure after Bud does his scientific Exacto knife analysis," Shorty replied. "But are you fellas thinking what I'm thinking?"

"How would we know that?" Howie asked. "We're not psychic."

"That would be telepathic, not psychic, Howie," Bud replied. "But Shorty, if you're thinking this Mason guy has nothing to do with real fossils coming out of the Tetons, I'll have to agree. In fact, I'm wondering if someone didn't help themselves to a bunch of his 3D fossils here in the museum to sell as the real deal. And it wouldn't surprise me if this was the source of the fossils Parker gave to the guy at the Mystery House."

"So, you think this Mason guy is innocent?" Howie asked.

"Innocent of selling fossils, maybe, especially if he values science like his wife says. But I'm beginning to think he may have something else up his sleeve."

"What would that be?" Shorty asked.

"Poaching," Bud replied. "And not just any old game, but game from Grand Teton National Park."

"I was kind of thinking the same thing," Shorty replied.

Howie said, "Sounds pretty serious, but I have a question."

"Shoot," Bud replied.

"What's a docent?"

Bud grinned, saying, "Howie, everybody knows what that is. Shorty, want to tell him?"

Shorty replied, "I know what it is because I've spent a lot of time in museums. A docent is a volunteer who does tours or answers questions, that sort of thing." He grinned. "Does that jive with what you know, Bud?"

Bud replied, "Sure. We have docents back at the River Museum in Green River, but we just call them volunteers. But fellas, it's about time for us to go home, I mean back to Green River, but we first need to go see what's going on at Fossil Mountain. It's too late to go today, but let's plan on it bright and early tomorrow morning."

"That's a plan," Howie said. "But since everyone else left and we're on our own, let's go to the Royal Magpie and have dinner one last time."

"Now *that's* a plan," Shorty said, nodding his head in agreement. "I've heard they have good food, though I can't say I've eaten there before."

"You *have* eaten there before," Howie said. "Though the *there* wasn't actually there, and that's all I'm gonna say about that."

They got in Bud's FJ, where Lindie patiently waited, gnawing on a wishbone-shaped chewie Wilma Jean had left her. She wagged her tail, and Bud wondered what the next day would bring for them all, again wishing he could've just gone on home with the gang.

Bud watched as Lindie chased a squirrel up a small aspen, then turned and waited for him to catch up. Shorty was a good quarter-mile ahead, while Howie was about that same distance behind, leaving Bud wondering whether he should hurry up or slow down.

Choosing the latter, he stopped, sitting on a big log, taking off his day pack while thinking about what he'd read on the Internet the previous evening about the Darby Canyon Wind Cave Trail. It had gone something like:

> *This six-mile round-trip hike has 1800 feet of elevation gain, which means the way back is all downhill! You start on an easy stroll by a creek through a beautiful meadow and are soon trying to catch your breath climbing uphill. Good luck if you're at all out of shape, as you'll need all the luck you can muster. This is considered one of the best Teton Valley hikes.*

He was thinking that maybe the part about needing good luck if you're out of shape was something he'd added in his mind while actually on the trail, as well as it being all downhill on the way back.

Lindie had dipped into the small creek and was now at Bud's feet shaking, getting his pant legs wet, but he didn't mind. He was glad to have her along, for she was a good bear alarm, and along with the can of bear spray in its holster on his belt, he hoped she would keep the bears away or at the very least alert him if one was near.

Bud thought back to the Internet guide again:

You will ascend more than 1,200 feet in less than two miles. As you climb, the views of the Jedediah Smith Wilderness get better and better. At the half-way point, you can see the massive cave entrance in the distance. It was here that we saw a bear across the ravine on the other side of the canyon. To top it off, a stream runs out of the cave to a beautiful waterfall.

He must not even be half-way, Bud decided, for he couldn't yet see the cave. Since it was around three miles one-way, half of that would be about one and a half miles, but it felt like they'd gone at the very least four or five miles. At this rate, he would never make it up to Fossil Mountain. He knew he'd be glad to have pictures later, but he was somewhat regretting taking his camera along, as it just added to the weight.

Howie, having finally caught up to Bud, said, "Man, Sheriff, at this rate, we'll never make it to the top. Being back home sitting on the porch drinking coffee sounds pretty good right now, especially since it's barely dawn."

"We did get an early start," Bud replied. "Which is good, considering the speed we're going. But at least my feet don't hurt."

"These boots are worth every penny right now," Howie replied. "Do you think there are wolves up here?"

"Without a doubt," Bud grinned.

Howie asked, "Where's Shorty? Should he be hiking alone?"

"Somewhere way ahead," Bud replied. "I doubt if a wolf would want to tangle with someone carrying a rock hammer. But I'm sure he'll wait for us at some point, though that point might be Fossil Mountain."

They continued on as the trail crossed the creek, then began climbing multiple switchbacks, soon passing a memorial for five hikers that had been killed by lightning. Crimson fireweed grew everywhere, seeming to give the landscape a faint ruby glow as the sun rose. Before long, they could make out a long line of cliffs on the skyline with a dark narrow slit in them.

"That looks pretty ominous," Howie said. "Must be the cave."

"That means we're barely halfway," Bud remarked. "And we're supposed to climb all the way to the top and then some?"

Just then, they heard a voice calling out, "Shorty, Shorty!"

Soon, they could make out someone coming up the trail as Lindie wagged her tail.

"It's Jamie McKenzie!" Bud said. "How did he know Shorty was up here?"

"Remember how Shorty said Cam wanted to come with us?" Howie said. "I bet he couldn't make it and substituted Jamie—and Shorty obviously forgot to tell us."

Upon catching up with them, Jamie looked surprised, saying somewhat suspiciously, "I didn't expect to see you two up here. Have you seen a guy named Shorty Doyle? Kind of tall and thin, grayish hair?"

"He's up ahead a ways," Howie replied. "Are you going to arrest him? If so, he won't go easy."

Jamie looked puzzled. "Did he do something wrong?"

"I don't think he has a parks pass," Howie replied. "And he's headed straight for the park."

Jamie, looking incredulous, walked past them and on up the trail. After he was gone, Bud started laughing as Howie said, "Well, it seems like he's out to arrest everyone, so I was just helping him out, Sheriff."

"I don't think he realizes we're all part of the same party," Bud replied. "He'll figure it out. But I hope those guys wait up for us, as Shorty said we leave this trail at some point and skirt the base of the cliffs until we come to a saddle, and from there on it's just a gentle slope on up to Fossil Mountain."

"If that's the case, we can probably just eyeball our way up," Howie offered. "Though it would be nice not to get separated."

"Agreed," Bud said. "But there they are, Howie."

Shorty and Jamie waited ahead by the trail, and when Bud and Howie finally reached them, Shorty said, "I know you guys have all met before, so let's just keep going on up the mountain. Jamie says this is a good place to leave the trail and freelance."

"You won't arrest us for going off-trail, will you?" Howie asked.

Jamie, looking irritated, turned off the trail and started towards the base of the cliffs that held the cave. As everyone followed, Howie whispered, "I'm kind of enjoying my own little form of retribution, Sheriff. Let me know if I'm overdoing it."

"Actually, I'm enjoying it, too," Bud replied. "But what I'm not enjoying is getting this tired. How far do you think we've come?"

Shorty, overhearing him, replied, "Maybe three miles, Bud. We still have a long ways to go, as it's about five miles to the saddle below the mountain. But I think it's easier hiking from here on out, except for those occasional scree fields. Lindie looks like she's doing fine."

"She stays in shape playing ball," Bud replied. "If I could get her to throw it to me once in awhile, I'd be in better shape myself."

Jamie led them up across the upper slopes of a broad high valley, stopping to inform them that they were at the head of the South Fork of Darby Canyon. He turned and continued on before Howie could ask another question.

"Dang it, Bud, I wanted to ask him what kind of flowers these were," Howie moaned. "There's sure a lot of them."

"I know those tall blue ones are lupine, and the red are Indian paintbrush," Bud replied. "And there's some kind of purple daisies and white columbine, and of course, fireweed."

"They're as thick as weeds," Howie exclaimed. "I guess that's why they call it fireweed. I've never seen so much color!"

Jamie led them to a saddle that broke through the cliffs, and as they finally reached its top, they could see they were at the base of Fossil Mountain. Steep talus fields led to the summit.

Jamie and Shorty had stopped and sat down, taking their lunches from their packs.

"This is a good place to have lunch," Shorty informed them, taking out a thermos of hot coffee. "Even though it's actually about breakfast time. Maybe Jamie can tell us a little about this part of the park."

Jamie replied, "We're not actually in the park yet, though we're very close. The boundary is just on this side of the Teton Crest Trail."

"What are those mountains way over there?" Shorty asked.

"That's Housetop and Rendezvous," Jamie replied, biting into a sandwich.

Howie asked, "Why is it called Fossil Mountain?"

Jamie frowned, then said, "Because of the abundance of small fossils near its summit."

"Only near the summit?" Howie persisted. "Because it looks like someone's been digging over there. See those pock marks in the shale?"

As he spoke, they heard a whoosh, and a glider suddenly filled the sky immediately above them, coming up from the opposite side of Fossil Mountain.

Jamie stood as the glider buzzed them, watching as it then turned and sailed on toward the Grand Teton.

"For once I got his tail number," Jamie said, writing it down on a notebook from his shirt pocket.

"Are gliders illegal over the park?" Howie asked.

"Like all manned aircraft, glider pilots must maintain a minimum altitude of 2,000 feet above the surface of national parks and monuments. He was no more than 100 feet above us, if that. I've seen this guy flying low before and wasn't able to ID him, until now, that is."

"Are there ever crashes in these big peaks?" Howie persisted.

Jamie, again looking irritated, replied, "Occasionally, but it's somewhat rare. The most famous was in November of 1950 when a C-47 cargo plane crashed on Mount Moran during a storm, killing all 21 on board."

"Oh, wow," Howie said. "I've never heard of that."

"People down in the valley saw a fire on the mountain and at first thought it was a forest fire until they realized it was above timberline and in the snow. The extreme location of the crash made it impossible to recover the plane or the bodies."

"It's still up there?" Howie asked.

"Yes, it's still there. The Park Service discourages climbs to the site."

Howie was quiet, and Bud figured he probably was through asking questions.

Still watching the glider, which had now barely cleared a nearby ridge, Shorty noted, "He looks to me like he's having trouble, like he's trying to find a thermal."

"Things don't look so good," Howie said as the glider turned again, barely clearing the top of Fossil Mountain. "I wonder if it's Mason."

Jamie said, "If he'd just head down Darby Canyon, he could probably make it to the Driggs Airport."

"I think that's what he's trying to do," Shorty replied as the glider appeared to be heading their way. "But he's too low to clear the pass. I think he's going to crash, boys."

Bud started to take out his camera, but thinking of Jamie's description of the crash on Mount Moran, changed his mind.

The last thing he wanted to remember his vacation by was a photo of a wrecked glider. He closed his eyes and hoped the glider would gain some lift and head for Driggs, leaving them to the peace and quiet of the big peaks.

32

It happened so fast that when trying to recollect exactly how it had all come down, Bud had trouble, for all he could remember was the adrenaline rush he felt upon realizing the glider was heading straight for them.

For a moment, he thought it might actually make it over the ridge, which would put it on the Darby Canyon side, but at the last possible second, it dipped and hit just below them.

Though Bud didn't actually see it, he later described the sound of the crash as one of the most disturbing things he'd ever heard, kind of like a combine hitting a large rock. Lindie must've also found it disturbing, he mused, for she had tried to get inside Bud's jacket—even though he was wearing it.

They were all quickly on their feet, and as he looked down the ridge, Bud expected to see smoke, but then remembered a sailplane had no engine. Instead of smoke, all was deathly quiet, the nose of the glider embedded in the tundra, having plowed it up as it came down.

Jamie was soon beside the glider, Shorty next to him, trying to open the canopy, which was severely cracked. Other than that and the buried nose, the plane was intact. Mason was inside, slumped over and looking as if he was either unconscious or possibly dead.

"It won't open!" Jamie yelled.

Howie and Bud were soon there, pulling on the canopy, but it was stuck shut.

Howie said, "We need to get inside and pull the canopy release knob."

He picked up a rock and hit the heavy plastic where it was cracked, which deformed it enough that he was able to stick his arm inside. Right next to where the canopy closed on the body of the glider was a lever, which he pulled.

The canopy detached from the fuselage, and they were able to lift it clear. Howie said, "Mason was showing me stuff when I took the flight with him. This knob is so the pilot can eject in case of emergency."

"It's too bad he didn't eject," Jamie said. "But we need to get him out of the plane before it starts sliding down the mountain. Any of you know first-aid?"

Bud said, simply, "I do."

He and Jamie carefully pulled Mason from the cockpit, trying not to injure him further, then carried him to the nearby top of the ridge, where they gingerly put him down.

Jamie pulled a first-aid kit from his pack, then handed it to Bud saying, "Can you check his vitals while I get a chopper in here?"

Bud quickly felt to see if Mason had a pulse, then said, "He's still alive and has a good heartbeat. There's no blood anywhere, so I'm guessing a concussion, though there may be internal injuries."

Jamie pulled out a GPS, took a reading, then took a satellite phone from his pack and made a call. Bud could tell that, as a ranger, this was something he'd done many times before.

After talking awhile, Jamie hung up and said, "Search and Rescue are on it, and we'll have a chopper here ASAP. We need to keep him as warm and as stable as possible. Shorty, can you scope out a good landing spot for the chopper?"

Bud took off his jacket and put it over Mason, who lay deathly still, then again checked his pulse, hoping the chopper would arrive soon. He knew Jamie was unaware that he had extensive training in both first-aid and search and rescue, but he felt no need to tell him.

As a former field geologist, Shorty had plenty of experience with helicopters, and he soon determined the chopper would be able to land on a nearby flat area.

As they silently waited, they soon heard a sound coming from the other side of the ridge. They at first thought it was the chopper, but upon looking over the edge, they could see the glider was slowly sliding down the steep mountainside.

"How will they get it out of here?" Howie asked Jamie.

"They'll have to cut it into pieces and take it out on mules," Jamie replied. "It won't be cheap."

"Who pays for it?" Howie persevered.

"I actually don't know," Jamie replied. "This isn't in the park, so I'm guessing it's national forest and they'll make the pilot pay for it."

Before long, they could hear the whoop-whoop of a distant helicopter, and as it came nearer, Shorty signaled where it should land, then stood back. It was soon on the ground, two EMTs jumping out and quickly assessing Mason, who appeared to be waking up. They soon had him on a gurney and back in the chopper, signaling for Jamie to get in.

"I need to ride out with this guy, but thanks for all your help," Jamie said. "It's been nice to have a competent team for all this."

"Wait a sec," Bud said. He knew it was bad timing, but he wasn't sure if he would see Jamie again, and it felt like a seize the moment kind of thing. "I think this is the guy you've been looking for. It looks like he's going to survive, and I hate to make his day worse, but if you go to his house, you'll find what you need to indict him. You may want to do a DNA test, assuming you can still match the head with the rest of the body. His name's Mason Barry, and he lives in the Teewinot Subdivision in Alta."

Jamie, looking puzzled, replied, "I'm not sure I follow you."

Bud said, "You know, discharging a firearm in a national park, disposing of a body, and all that stuff you tried to arrest us for."

Jamie, though surprised, nodded his head, then repeated the words *Mason Barry, Teewinot."*

As Jamie turned to board the chopper, Bud said, "I almost forgot —one more thing. Cam has the plaque you've been looking for."

Jamie, looking dazed, as if he was unable to process it all, quickly boarded the chopper, and they were off.

"What was that all about, Sheriff?" Howie asked.

"I'll explain later," Bud replied. "We need to go take a look at those pock marks you spotted before it gets dark."

"Don't look now, but it looks like somebody else is interested in them, too," Shorty replied, pointing at two distant figures.

Bud said, "I have a hunch we already know who that is. Let's go pay them a visit."

Just as he said this, they heard a crash, and investigating, they could see that the glider had slid on down the mountain, crumpling into the rocks below.

"Looks like Mason won't be having to cut that thing into pieces before carting it out after all," Howie said. "That should save him a little cash. How far do you think it is down there?"

"Far enough," Shorty replied.

"That's not very accurate," Howie complained.

Shorty replied, "Far enough is a good enough measure. It works fine for horseshoes and hand grenades, so why not gliders? But let's go see who's out here digging illegal fossils."

33

"It's better to regret the things you've done, than regret those you haven't," a woman's voice said, a voice that Bud recognized as Winnie's. "I wonder what that chopper was all about."

"But Winnie," said a second voice. "Isn't it illegal to collect fossils like this?"

Bud knew it was Georgie. The pair was back, and it seemed they were at it again, rock hammers in hand and packs ready to be filled.

"I don't know how to protect them other than digging them up, do you?" Winnie asked.

"We can never dig all these up," Georgie replied incredulously.

Bud, Howie, and Shorty stood at the base of a small ridge made of layers of shale that eventually merged with a larger ridge at the base of Fossil Mountain. Even though the trio had made no effort to hide, the women were so busy they hadn't noticed them standing a mere 20 feet below.

The women each had rock hammers and would strike a layer of shale until a piece broke off, then they'd use the hammer to pry the shale into two parts, the fossils revealing themselves between the thin layers. Some pieces bore nothing, and they would casually toss them over their shoulders.

"What would these sell for?" Georgie asked.

"I'm not sure," Winnie replied. "But I'm sure it depends on the actual fossil and who buys them. I've seen them online from several hundred dollars up into the tens of thousands of dollars, depending on how rare they are and the quality."

"How are we going to keep someone else from stealing them?" Georgie asked. "We can't put an armed guard up here, and a number of people must come by here to cross Fossil Pass on their way to Alaska Basin. It's a popular hike."

Winnie stopped hammering and turned to Georgie, looking directly at her. "We can't stop them. That's why we need to get as many out as we can. We can keep coming back until we can't, then maybe put rocks and dirt over where we've dug to hide it."

"What if a park ranger comes by?" Georgie asked.

"We're not in the park," Winnie replied. "There's nothing they can do. But it's late afternoon and we need to finish loading our packs and get going. I really don't want to try to go down the Devil's Staircase in the dark."

"It's way too far to go down Teton Canyon—I mean, miles farther. We need to go back the way we came, through Darby."

"Are you sure, Georgie? Isn't that the way you and Jill came out the other day?"

"No, we came down Darby. You're going to add miles onto the trek by going down Teton. We wouldn't get in until midnight, if then."

"OK, we'll go back down Darby," Winnie replied.

Bud was amazed they hadn't noticed them yet, but that was soon to end, for Winnie tossed a piece of shale over her shoulder which hit Howie smack on his arm.

"Ow! Watch where you're tossing stuff," he said, irritated.

Winnie turned, surprised, nearly tumbling down the steep slope just as Lindie, who was standing by Bud, began whining, then started pacing around Bud's legs.

It was but moments later he could feel a strange oscillation, as if some kind of wave was passing through him, which was followed by a loud boom. Bud stood in shock as that was followed by a crack like a rifle shot.

"Get out of the rocks!" He yelled, and Howie and Shorty ran away from the cliff and back down to the saddle. Winnie and Georgie likewise came sliding down and ran after them.

Rocks came tumbling down the face of the mountain as they watched in shock, a dust cloud rising. The quake was short-lived, and finally, when it seemed as if the last rock had clattered down, Bud said, "I think that's a sign it's quitting time."

"That was a close call," Winnie said with excitement.

"Did you feel that weird oscillation?" Bud asked.

Shorty said, "Those were probably p-waves, Bud, or the primary waves of an earthquake. And I noticed Lindie acting odd—animals can sense low-frequency Rayleigh waves that accompany earthquakes and can serve as an early-warning system."

"Good little doggie, Lindie," Bud said, patting her head and calming her down. "You made up for chewing up my yoyo. I'm glad everyone's OK."

"It's time to head home," Shorty said. "Are you gals going with us?"

Winnie replied, "We need to get our packs and rock hammers, but I'm afraid to go back over there. What are you guys doing out here, anyway?"

"We could ask you the same thing," Shorty replied. "But that was just a small quake, Winnie, maybe about a 3.0. Quakes that small don't usually have aftershocks. I'll go get your stuff. It's getting late and we need to get down out of here."

"We got a late start," Georgie said nervously, then as Shorty went up the hill to get their packs, Howie following, she asked Bud, "Did you see what we're doing? You won't tell anyone, will you?"

Bud replied, "I'm not sure if digging fossils here is legal or not. Shorty's a geologist on contract with the park, and I doubt if you can get him to keep mum about it."

"For the millionth time, Georgie, we're not in the park," Winnie replied. "We're on private land."

"Don't you mean forest service land?" Bud asked.

"No," Winnie replied. "Private land. It's an inholding."

Bud could see Howie and Shorty had climbed up to where Winnie and Georgie had been digging and were looking closely at the layers. Shorty got down on his hands and knees, then, looking all around, appeared to be very excited. He and Howie picked up the packs and rock hammers, then came back down, and Bud could tell he was beside himself.

"I think we may have a lagerstätte here, Bud," he said excitedly. "As far as I can see, layer after layer of Burgess Shale type fossils. It's absolutely incredible!"

"You guys," Georgie said. "I think Winnie's having trouble."

Winnie was now sitting on the ground, her head tilted forward, crying. Georgie sat down next to her, putting her arm around her shoulders, saying, "It's Marty, isn't it?" Winnie seemed unable to talk, so Georgie just sat with her as she sobbed.

Bud, feeling helpless, watched as Lindie went to the woman and began licking her hand. Winnie looked up and stopped crying as she stroked Lindie's head over and over.

Finally, she said, "I'm sorry. All those rocks coming down brought back a very painful memory." Standing, she added, "I'm OK now."

"I hope whatever it was gets better," Bud said.

They could see the sun was getting low and would soon set. Bud turned to look at the mountains behind them, which were now draped in a deep crimson alpenglow that seemed to be melting down the mountainsides.

For a brief moment, Bud was struck by how incredible the Tetons were, and how amazing it really was that the fossil remnants of life millions of years ago existed, some of it right here. He tried to picture how everything was once the bottom of an ocean with these strange little creatures swimming around, living their lives day by day, unaware of the deep time that stretched back for eons.

As they all started back down Darby Canyon, he felt a sudden surge of happiness, glad that he'd came here, even though he'd been missing his home back in Green River. It had been an experience like nothing else, and it had served to strengthen his friendships.

And best of all, he felt he now had what he needed to answer all the questions that had been plaguing him since they'd first arrived at the Teewinot Cafe.

34

Bud and Winnie sat in the kitchen of the Teewinot Cafe, drinking tea and finishing the last of a coffee cake Wilma Jean had left for them. They'd gotten back late, having to navigate the lower part of Darby Canyon by flashlight, which hadn't been too bad, as the trail was easy to follow.

Georgie had gone on home, and Shorty and Howie had gone to bed. Lindie sat at Bud's feet, waiting for a bite of the cake, Bud finally letting her lick the last of the crumbs from the paper plate he'd been using.

"You're welcome to come stay in the house now," Bud said. "You can have Doc and Millie's room."

"Have you heard from them?" She asked. "Did they get back OK?"

"They got back a few hours before we did," Bud replied. "My wife was kind of panicked because I didn't answer the phone, but we finally got together. It's been a long day for everyone. How did Bijou fare?"

"Oh, he's fine. All he does is sleep all day, anyway. Thanks for the offer, but I'm pretty much at home in my VW, so I'll just stay out there. They should be opening the campground back up in a day or two."

Bud nodded, then, patting Lindie's head, asked, "Say, Winnie, not to pry, but do you mind sharing with me what memory the earthquake triggered—was it something about Marty?"

He suspected he knew the answer, but he wanted to hear what Winnie had to say. He added, "If you don't want to talk about it, it's OK, but I think it had something to do with that rockfall, didn't it? I mean, you've mentioned rockfall several times. Was that what killed him?"

Winnie was quiet for some time, but finally, said, "I don't know if I should talk about it or not, but it would be nice to get it off my chest. I've just been too afraid, that's all."

"Afraid of what?"

"Actually, afraid of being arrested."

"What?" Bud asked incredulously. "Did you do something illegal? Does it have to do with the fossils?"

"No," she replied. "It doesn't have anything to do with the fossils. Georgie's kind of a basket case. I told her we were OK, since I own the land, but she kept worrying. I wish I had some way to keep people off it."

Bud, not really sure what to say, said, "You said it was a private inholding, but I didn't realize you owned it. Was this Marty's mining claim by any chance?"

"Yes, and he left it to me. Parker's been wanting to buy it, but Marty wouldn't sell it to him, as Parker wanted to build a resort up there. As you know, it has fantastic views, and it actually shares a border with the park. I've been up there with Marty many times."

"Did Marty know about the fossils?" Bud asked.

"Yes, though I don't think he realized how rare they were. There are fossils all over up there, even in the rocks as you're climbing up Darby Canyon, but they're not the rare kind like on the claim. But Bud, I've made an important decision about it."

Bud sighed. He felt she was getting farther and farther away from telling him anything about Marty's death, though it did occur to him that she really didn't know anything about it.

She continued. "As you know, it borders Grand Teton National

Park. It's an old claim from the late 1800s, and since it was private, the park boundary had to honor that when they created the park in 1929. It's a patented mining claim, which means the Federal Government has given its title to the claimant, which includes both the minerals and the surface, so it's like owning private land and you can build on it. The original park included only the Teton Range and six glacial lakes at the base of the mountains, and though that boundary was established back then, a bunch of land has been added since."

"Interesting," Bud remarked.

"As we were hiking down Darby Canyon, I realized that the only way that area could be preserved is by adding it to the park. I'm going to donate it. And if what Shorty told me on the way down is true, that he suspects it's a—what did he call it?"

"A lagerstätte," Bud offered.

"Yes, that, and he says it may be of international importance in the paleontological world. I'm going to call Cam tomorrow and start the proceedings to donate it, and then hopefully the park can create some kind of protection for it, as well as open it to actual paleontologists who know what they're doing. And I want them to name it after Marty."

"That's awesome, Winnie. Did you tell Shorty?"

"Yes, when we were hiking down. He helped me realize how important it could be."

She was quiet, then said, "I'm exhausted. I need to go to bed. Shorty also told me about the glider crashing. I guess that happened just before Georgie and I got up there. It was too late to be hiking up the canyon, but I had to wait for her to get off work. I've been kind of obsessed about getting as many of the fossils out as we could."

"Thanks for sharing all that, Winnie," Bud said. "I guess I'll go to bed. It's been quite a day."

"Agreed," Winnie replied. "Shorty said that now that everyone knows where the fossil site is and I'm going to donate it, you guys will be going home soon."

"Probably in a day or two when we get rested up," Bud replied.

"I may have to come down your way when I go back to my daughter's in Utah, though I won't be spending as much time down there as before."

"Why not?"

"Marty left me his house. His daughter got his investments, which are pretty substantial, so she's happy for me. She has a nice place and wasn't interested in it."

"Where's his house, Winnie?"

"It's here in Alta. Only about a half-mile from the old cafe here. It has stunning views of the Grand. He knew I'd think about him and his great-grandfather climbing the peak, it being right there out his living-room window."

"That's awesome, Winnie. I hope you can get down our way."

They sat in silence, and Bud was about to get up and go to bed, when from nowhere, Winnie said, "Alright, I'll tell you the rest."

She sighed, then continued. "Marty came by one day asking me to climb Teewinot with him. We both had done a lot of climbing together in our younger days, and Marty still did some as part of his ranger job. I used to climb a lot—I've done the Grand several times and a lot of the other big peaks. When I was younger, I wanted to do nothing but climb. He knew I'd climbed Teewinot, and he wanted me to go with him, as he had this plaque he'd had made that said his great-grandfather was the first to climb it. He wanted to put it up there to memorialize him."

She continued, "I have no idea if his great-grandfather was actually the first, but I agreed to go along, mostly because I was worried about something happening to him. I can see the irony in it now, because without me, he'd probably still be alive. At first, Teewinot's just a steep hike, but once you get above the Worshipper and Idol, which are huge rock towers, the trail turns into scree fields and huge boulders, which makes the route-finding difficult. There's an area called the Narrows that you have to get up and over, and it has a fair amount of exposure. The Narrows makes you pause because you're 4,000 feet above the valley."

She stopped, then continued on while petting Lindie. "Marty had trouble there, but we finally got on through. He seemed to kind of be losing his nerve, and I can't say I blame him. We got to the top, taking turns because it's too small to hold two people, and what a thrill that was, but it was then that he realized there was no place to really attach a plaque. He decided to cram it between some slabs near the top, and we headed back down.

"Statistically, this is the most deadly climb in the Tetons, and mostly because route finding here is very difficult. We finally got almost all the way down, and I could see some other climbers coming up, so I stayed behind and let Marty go ahead. He passed me, then I started down. We should've been wearing helmets, but we weren't. As I started down, I heard a boom, like a big firecracker almost, and all of a sudden a bunch of rocks broke loose and went right smack down on Marty. They left a hollowed-out place so I couldn't get down. After the rockfall stopped, the other climbers ran to where Marty was and started first aid, and then one of them took off back down the trail, I assume to call for help.

"I didn't know what to do. I was stuck, but I felt like it was my fault that the rocks came down, but now I wonder if it wasn't from an earthquake. I'm not big enough to knock a bunch like that down. I watched as the rangers prepared Marty's body for extraction by helicopter longline. I found out later that they took Marty to the Lupine Meadows Rescue Cache and transferred his body to the Teton County Coroner.

"It was almost dark by then, and I managed to find a way to chimney down, almost falling in the effort, and as I got to the parking lot, I could hear one of the climbers talking to a ranger and telling them someone had knocked the slab down by being careless. The ranger was taking a statement and ended up telling the climber that that person, who of course was me, could be charged with manslaughter.

"I read later that manslaughter is when you didn't plan the crime or intend for the victim to die, but you caused an accident that resulted in someone else's death. I went home in shock, too scared to tell anyone. You're the first person I've talked to about it."

Bud sighed. "That's quite the story. You probably don't know this, but I'm the sheriff of a pretty large county down in Utah. It doesn't have a lot of residents, but we get a lot of outdoorsy tourists, and a lot of them are climbers. What happened to Marty isn't unusual, and I don't know of one case where a manslaughter charge has been filed. Rockfall and such things are just considered part of the risk."

Winnie hugged Lindie to her, and Bud could tell she was crying. After awhile, she dried her eyes, stood, and went over and hugged Bud.

"Thank you," she said, then added, "Tell Jamie what I just told you if you see him. I'm worried to death about what will become of Bijou if I go to prison."

"Winnie, you won't go to prison, but if anything happens, you can be assured Wilma Jean and I would take care of Bijou until you came back."

Winnie nodded, then went to her VW bus.

35

It was a couple of days later, and Bud, Howie, and Shorty all sat at a table in the Royal Magpie, Cam and Jamie across from them. They would be leaving soon, but Cam had wanted to treat them all to a nice lunch before they left.

They'd been talking about Marty's mining claim, and Bud could tell both Jamie and Cam were excited.

Cam said, "Well, Shorty, you certainly came through on this one. I can't thank you enough for all you've done. Marty's claim is going to make a really nice addition to the park and its resources."

"Thank Bud and Howie," Shorty said. "They're the ones who worked their way through all this. I just went along for the ride."

"And what a ride it was," Jamie laughed. "By the way, I have an arrest warrant out for Mason. We've been after him for some time for flying too low in the park. I hope he's learned his lesson."

"Is he OK?" Bud asked.

"It was like you said," Jamie replied. "A concussion. He's home now. I visited him yesterday afternoon. He's doing fine. He's lucky he wasn't killed."

"That was nice of you to go see him," Howie said. "But you're going to actually arrest him for flying too low?"

"Well, his health wasn't exactly why I was there, nor was his reckless flying," Jamie replied. "I was getting a DNA sample from the elk head Bud told me about hanging on his wall. I'm pretty convinced it's going to match the body we recovered from that grave over on Teewinot, plus he confessed to shooting it. He knows he's in big trouble."

"So, he shot the elk in the park, then took just the head and tried to hide the body by burying it?" Shorty asked.

"Exactly. He'd been using his glider to spot animals, then, once he knew the general area they were in, would go hunt them. That elk was an icon in the park. He hung around Lupine Meadows a lot and gave a lot of people a thrill seeing and photographing him. It's a high-profile case, and he's going to pay a stiff penalty, as well as probably spend some time in jail."

Bud asked, "So, when you accused us of all those crimes, it was all pertaining to the elk? I wondered when I found the elk hair in the grave, but I was stuck on the idea of the grave having something to do with Marty's death."

Cam replied, "Mason shot the elk in the park, which is the discharging a firearm charge. He then transported the head through the park to a taxidermist, which is the transporting stolen material charge, and we've already talked to the taxidermist, who has implicated Mason. Disposing of a body and theft of government property are charges from trying to hide the elk's body and from illegally taking wildlife within a national park."

"I really apologize for thinking you guys did it," Jamie said. "It's just that you fit the bill—the entrance-station camera showed a 4 by 4 vehicle with Utah plates."

"You couldn't read the number on the plates or see exactly what kind of vehicle?" Shorty asked.

"No, the light was really poor from blowing dust," Jamie replied. "Once again, I'm sorry. I was being a bit overzealous. That bull elk was one of my favorites. I've spent hours watching him. I know now that Mason has a vehicle that fits. But you put a scare in me when you said the grave was Marty's. I didn't know he was dead at that point, just missing. Marty and I had worked together quite a bit when I was an interp, so I was shocked."

"What's an interp?" Howie asked.

"An interpretive ranger," Jamie replied. "The ones who tell you about the park, as opposed to those who arrest you for ignorance about the park. I was an interp before I became an LEO. And yes, I did catch on that you were trying to get revenge with all your questions, and I guess I deserved it."

"That fossil in the grave was pretty much what led us to Mason," Bud said. "But did you guys interview the hikers who said they saw it all come down, I mean the rockfall that killed Marty?"

"How do you know about witnesses?" Jamie asked. "Yes, I did talk to the climbers that found Marty, but they didn't know who the person above him in the rocks was. It's too circumstantial to even begin to make a case. The coroner said a blow to the head, and he was in the middle of rockfall when he was found. There's no question that that's what killed him, but we just had to be sure and follow any leads."

"Good to know," Bud said, now certain he didn't need to mention Winnie. It was better to let it be, since there was no way she was guilty. He'd tell her later not to worry.

Howie asked Jamie, "Are you and Cam related?"

Jamie laughed, "Another question, eh? Yes, he's my father-in-law. I married his wonderful daughter."

"Is that why you wanted Bud and Howie off the case?" Shorty asked, turning to Cam.

"Pretty much," Cam replied. "I didn't suspect Jamie of doing anything wrong, but I was worried that, since he was in the middle of everything, things might point his direction by coincidence. I wanted time to figure it all out before outsiders got involved. It's part of the negative scenario of working with relatives, though Jamie was a ranger long before he married my daughter. And on top of all that, everyone knew he and Marty were feuding about that dang plaque, which is in the museum now, by the way. A lot of folks were happy to see it returned."

"Cam, we understand perfectly," Bud said. "And I suspected as much. But has there been any report on why Mason crashed his glider?"

Cam replied, "Since he crashed on the park boundary, we are working on a report, or I should say, Jamie is. Have you found anything so far?"

Jamie replied, "I was out at the glider place at the airport this morning, and they told me—well, here, let me read my notes, because it's mostly Greek to me."

He pulled a small notebook from his shirt pocket and said, "It sounded to them like Mason was trying to ridge soar his sailplane down low on the western base of the Tetons, but he got shot down from sink and strong winds. He did pretty good at staying aloft and not getting boxed in, but the winds down low were flowing around the mountains instead of up over them. This created some exciting but difficult wind shadows and produced very little lift down low. The turbulence was pretty strong down low but they think he got hit by an unexpected wind sheer at the wrong moment."

"What's sink?" Howie asked.

"I don't know," Jamie replied. "Probably exactly what it sounds like."

Just then, Parker came in the door. Bud figured he must know Jamie and Cam, as he came by and said, "You fellas need to get ready for a nice lodge right there by Fossil Mountain. You can stop by when you're doing backcountry patrol and I'll give you a free cup of coffee."

"You're never going to get that claim," Jamie said.

"I'm working on it right now," Parker replied.

"You better hurry on over to park headquarters, 'cause we're working on annexing it as we speak," Cam grinned. "Winnie just deeded it to the park."

"You have to be kidding," Parker replied angrily.

Howie said, "Mr. Parker, I think you made a big mistake in buying the Mystery House."

"How so?" Parker asked.

"Weren't you aware that all mystery houses are built on vortices?"

Howie said. "I mean, you can't build on a vortex. You didn't do your homework on that one, did you?"

"You have to be kidding," Parker said.

"Not kidding," Howie replied.

"You mean a vortex is a real thing?"

"Yes," Howie answered as Bud tried to hide his grin. "Vortices are part of the world where the improbable is the commonplace and everyday physical facts are reversed. They're a challenge to accepted theories. Ask my friend Shorty, here. He has a PhD in science, he knows."

Parker, looking incredulous, said, "You have to be kidding."

Shorty replied, "He's right. Even science has no idea about vortices, but we all know you can't build in them. Looks like you bought a dud. Sit down and have a beer with us, and we'll help you drown your sorrows."

Parker turned to go, repeating one more time, "You have to be kidding," then walked out the door.

Jamie looked at Howie with admiration and said, "Well done, sir —very well done."

36

Bud sat in his old leather recliner in the bungalow, legs stretched out, with Hoppie in his lap and Pierre sleeping on his feet, his long little body about to fall off the footrest.

Lindie slept on the colorful handmade rag rug Wilma Jean had picked up years ago at the Green River second-hand store, the dog's legs twitching as she chased something in her sleep.

Bud's laptop was open, and he was slowly going through the photos he'd downloaded from their trip to the Tetons, enjoying every image. Sometimes he wondered if coming home and reliving the trip wasn't better than the actual trip itself, though he knew he couldn't savor the memories if he'd never made them in the first place.

They'd been back only a little over a week, but parts of the trip seemed like they were in the distant past, and he knew it was simply because he was getting back into the rhythm of life in the slow lane of Green River.

A lot of the trip had gone by much too fast, which seemed to be the nature of trying to solve mysteries, for by focusing on the facts of the case and trying to figure it all out, one wasn't as apt to notice the details that make up daily life, and for some reason, this made time go faster.

He studied a picture he'd taken of the Grand Teton, and he felt a sense of satisfaction in knowing that Jamie and his family could cherish their great-grandfather's role in Teton history by seeing the plaque in the park museum.

He was also glad that Winnie, along with Marty's daughter, would have the satisfaction of knowing that Marty would play a role in scientific history, a role even greater than his great-grandfather would have had by being the first to climb the Grand Teton, assuming he indeed had.

The Langford Lagerstätte had already made international news and would soon become the talk of Grand Teton National Park, especially once Cam established guided backcountry tours, and Bud suspected it would be making scientific history for some time, considering all the fossils still encased in its shales.

Bud carefully picked Pierre up, waking the little dog, then closed the recliner footrest, gently setting him on the floor. He could tell something was going on outside from the orange glow coming in through the windows, so he went into the back yard, the dogs following.

The Bookcliffs were on fire, their mighty ramparts lit with burgundy as the sun slowly drifted behind the rise of the distant San Rafael Swell.

He stood in silence as the glow began to fade, the earth's curvature making the light reflect higher onto the long narrow clouds above the Books, turning the clouds deep pinks and reds, then, as the sun dipped even farther, shades of amber.

Soon, the light was gone, the last trace of color fading as the sun slid even further into oblivion, everything turning shades of brown and gray.

Bud was glad he had noticed and gone outside to see the incredible sight, and even the dogs seemed pensive and quiet.

Going back inside, he fed the dogs their dinner, then again opened an envelope that Wilma Jean had brought home at lunch after stopping at the post office.

It was addressed to him and had a return address of Alta,

Wyoming, and as he read the note for a second time, he felt a sense of far-awayness, like he'd visited a land in a dream and couldn't quite put his finger on where it actually was.

Dear Bud,

Bijou says hello and wants you to have this photo. He would love for you and your wife and the pups to come visit some time.

I wanted you to know that Jamie says I'm nuts to have worried like I did, so everything's fine. He and I are actually friends now, but he says only as long as I don't beat him up. I think he's joking, but maybe not. Ha.

Parker wants to buy my old VW bus to live in (maybe not kidding), as he's being sued by the state because his Teton Flats building violates a bunch of code and it looks like he's going to lose a bunch of money.

We miss you and hope you enjoyed your time in our beautiful mountains.

All our best,

Winnie and Bijou

Bud looked at the photo she'd sent, a picture of Bijou curled up in a cat bed on a wide window sill, his fur glowing red just like Bud had seen the Books glowing moments before. Behind Bijou, visible through the window in the distance, stood the Grand Teton, its highest pinnacles lit with the same alpenglow that was making Bijou's fur glow red.

It was a stunning photo, a reminder of what makes life worth living, Bud thought, friends both furry and non, as well as country that would be forever wild.

He hoped he could take Winnie up on her invitation sometime, for he knew the mountains would always haunt him when he was here in the desert, just as the desert haunted him when in the high country.

He attached the photo to the fridge door with a magnet, grabbed a bowl of vanilla-bean ice cream, and headed out to the back porch with the dogs, where they would enjoy the balmy summer evening filled with the humming of crickets, waiting for Wilma Jean to come home from the cafe, hopefully with some kind of leftovers, preferably enchiladas. In the meantime, he would mess around with his new gift, another yoyo from Howie.

This one was a genuine Duncan Reflex Auto, which, according to the box, "Features technology that makes the yo-yo return to your hand automatically and that is especially recommended for kids under six years old because of how easy is is to learn with, all the while developing key fine motor skills and hand-eye coordination."

Life was good, he thought, as he walked out the back door and on to better things.

ABOUT THE AUTHOR

Chinle Miller writes from southeastern Utah and western Colorado, where she spends most of her time wandering with her dogs. She has an A.S. in Geology, a B.A. in Anthropology, and an M.A. in Linguistics.

If you enjoyed this book, you'll also enjoy Bud's look at his little town of Green River, Utah in *A Slice of Life in Watermelon Town,* as well as the other books in the Bud Shumway mystery series:

The Ghost Rock Cafe
The Slickrock Cafe
The Paradox Cafe
The No Delay Cafe
The Silver Spur Cafe
The Ice House Cafe
The Rattlesnake Cafe
The Beartooth Cafe
The Melon Rind Cafe
The Cessna Cafe
The Klondike Cafe
The Yellow Cat Cafe
The Swiftcurrent Cafe
The Sunnyside Cafe
The Temple Mountain Cafe
The Black Dragon Cafe
The Teewinot Cafe is the seventeenth book in this series.

And Chinle has a new series of national park books out for readers from age 8 on up, the first being *The Tuxedo Cat Kids in the*

Mystery of the Lost Arch (set in Arches), with fantastic artwork by Moab native Cary Cox.

Don't miss *Desert Rats: Adventures in the American Outback, Uranium Daughter, Wandering off the Map,* and *The Impossibility of Loneliness*, also by Chinle Miller.

And if you enjoy Bigfoot stories, you'll love *Rusty Wilson's Bigfoot Campfire Stories* and his many other Bigfoot books, as well as his popular *Chasing After Bigfoot: My Search for North America's Most Elusive Creature*.

Other offerings from Yellow Cat Publishing include an RV series by RV expert Sunny Skye, which includes *Living the Simple RV Life, The Truth about the RV Life,* and *RVing with Pets,* as well as *Tales of a Campground Host*. And don't forget to check out the books by Sunny's friend, Bob Davidson: *On the Road with Joe* and *Any Road, USA*. And finally, you'll love Roger Dean Miller's comedy thriller, *Bombing Hoffman*.

www.ingramcontent.com/pod-product-compliance
Lightning Source LLC
Chambersburg PA
CBHW020842260626
47169CB00003B/1097